The Voices of Julie

Joan L. Oppenheimer

SCHOLASTIC BOOK SERVICES
New York Toronto London Auckland Sydney Tokyo

To Ann Reit
With warm affection and
deep gratitude

ISBN: 0-590-05780-4

Copyright © 1979 by Joan Oppenheimer. All rights reserved. Published by Scholastic Book Services, a division of Scholastic Magazines, Inc.

12 11 10 9 8 7 6 5 4 3   9/7 0 1 2 3 4/8

Printed in the U.S.A.

01

The Voices of Julie

CHAPTER 1

Julie dreamed that night about the accident six years ago on a fog-shrouded freeway in which her parents lost their lives. The recurring dream featured two overlapping episodes. First, she would relive the moment when her mother screamed, and the little girl in the back seat woke to horror, seeing the collision with the cars ahead. Fifteen of them, she learned later, smashing into each other in the worst pileup of the decade on that road in southern California.

In the second part of the dream, Julie would find herself stumbling through cold clinging fog searching for her parents, sobbing as she heard them calling to her in voices shrill with terror.

She woke with tears on her face as she always did in the aftermath of a tormenting repetition of that sequence. Even when her conscious mind took over and she was once again aware of the

1

dream's distortion, she found it difficult to shake an ensuing heaviness of depression.

The next morning, still gripped by a somber mood, she got up and hurried to take a shower. Eyes closed, she gradually relaxed, as if the warm water were washing away the last lingering shreds of the web of nightmare. She finished with an icy spray that left her shivering as she toweled dry, but her spirits lifted as she had hoped.

For a moment, she stared at the steam-blurred reflection in the mirror, a small girl wrapped in a pink towel, another wound in a turban around her short blonde hair. Gray eyes dominated delicate features that lent themselves to a flexibility of moods, and an occasional devastating impression of someone else.

Looking at that face, indistinct now in the misted mirror, she recalled, with an icy constriction in her chest, the vivid agony of her dream. She snatched another towel from the rack and scrubbed frantically at the glass, caught again in the unreasoning fear evoked by fog.

Her reflection sharp and clear once more, she smiled ruefully. Symbolic, she thought, a blurred mirror for someone with self-image problems. She had been aware for some time that her confusion in that area was one reason, perhaps the most important one, for the impressions she did.

It had been a wonderful moment when she first discovered her gift for mimicry. It proved a marvelous way of hiding the seething insecurity that no one seemed to suspect. She never discussed it with anyone except her best friend, Teresa Martone. Even Teresa didn't realize the one thing Julie was sure of about her true self, whoever that might be. Reality almost certainly would be unacceptable to others. She would be unadmired, inadequate.

Her aunt Roslyn had never learned the extent of the problem, either. Roz didn't like to talk about anything negative, even to admit that a problem might exist, especially where Julie was concerned.

"Sugar," she would say, eyes warm, "with your looks and personality — and certainly your I.Q. too — you can do anything you set your mind to do. With all the new fields opening up to women and nobody at home tying you in knots with a lot of rigid unreasonable rules, *inhibiting* you — listen, luv, the sky's the limit."

It wasn't her aunt's fault if Julie didn't feel up to conquering all those worlds available beneath the heavens and stretching to the farthest horizon. For six years, Roz had done her best to be mother and father as well as adoring aunt, spoiling her rotten, doubtless. Yet Julie felt more and more the uneasiness of isolation, the only one in her crowd who didn't have to cope with a single rule or restriction. Well, that was part of her problem too.

Anybody would think she'd have it together at sixteen. Everybody else her age seemed to be functioning pretty well by now, unless they were into something like drugs to complicate matters. By the time she was dressed, however, she had managed to shrug off the invisible cloud of gloom that the dream always left in its wake.

It took only a few minutes to blow-dry her hair, and she ran a comb through the short bright curls, happy with her decision to cut her hair this summer. It hadn't worked any instant miracles, of course, bringing a nebulous self-image into focus. But then, she hadn't really hoped it would.

That kind of change took place deep inside a person. It would be great if it might be accomplished by way of a simple surgical procedure, she thought. She sighed, thinking about that, wishing it were that easy. Something like an appendectomy, perhaps, so she could pop in and out of the hospital, back in action within a week.

This being Saturday, she didn't bother with make-up. She never used much, anyway. But Mesa Verde, several miles inland from the ocean, had been sweltering in the usual October heat, so she applied a light film of moisturizer to her face and neck, hung her towels neatly on the rack, and went to get breakfast.

Today, she didn't pause by the pictures of her parents, Ann and Phillip Enright, propped on the what-not shelf by the door. She never stopped to talk to those smiling faces when she felt down about something. She might cry, and she hated it when she or anyone else cried. It was an admission of failure, somehow. Her parents would want her to be happy. That's what life was all about, finding happiness, having fun, being popular.

Halfway through her cereal and fruit, Roz appeared, wearing a short terrycloth robe and fuzzy scuffs. Her hair was a gleaming black cap, but her face seemed much too pale. It was something about older women that often puzzled Julie, the way it looked as if they had less blood in their faces. Without artificial color, they seemed washed out and tired even if they weren't.

An hour from now, Roz would emerge from the incredible litter of the blue-and-white master bathroom with the usual sparkle in her eyes, skin glowing with vitality and health, and whatever it was she had applied in there from a jar or bottle or tube. She would look at least ten years younger than the forty she admitted to, a little like the Elizabeth Taylor Julie had seen in early movies like *Giant*.

Except for a soft subdued "Morning, honey," her aunt didn't speak until she finished her juice and a mug of poisonous-looking black coffee.

Then she sighed and pushed the morning paper aside. "Nothing like the headlines to brighten your day," she said on a weary note. "Death and destruction and higher taxes. And one damned politician or another ranting about how we're going to hell in a handbasket if we don't do things his way." She studied her niece for a moment. "Have fun last night?"

Julie nodded. "Nick's okay. How was — " She lowered her voice, mimicking the slow drawl of her aunt's date for the evening, an amiable Texan " — call-me-Hal-honey?"

Roz laughed. "Oh, that's really good. I swear, I crack up every time you do that." She put her head to one side then, looking thoughtful. A three-time loser in the matrimonial market, she was candid these days about her search for Numero Cuatro. "Hal's a pretty good sort. Loaded, hopefully." Another small sigh. "Lord knows, I could overlook a whole bunch if the package included a fat healthy bank account."

Her niece looked at her, curious. George, Husband Number 1, who departed long before Julie came on the scene, had been prosperous by most people's standards. She barely remembered Eric, Number 2, but he had owned a small chain of variety stores. And Allen, who walked out a year ago, was a partner in the real estate firm where her aunt still worked.

It had been a friendly divorce, Roz insisted. Compared to the anger and bitterness with which she viewed the first two, perhaps it was. Julie had never felt comfortable with Allen because of his persistent attempts to be some kind of father figure. She remembered her own father very well, so that was the last thing she needed.

"What time did you get in?" Roz inquired now, but casually, not as if it were important.

"Just a little before you came in."

It had been late, almost two, but Roz merely nodded. It was the first thing she told Julie's dates, the fact that she didn't believe in curfews. She trusted Julie's judgment about such matters.

During the years while that judgment had been in a shaky formative stage, her aunt's permissive attitude had caused any number of problems. For Julie, dating had been frightening at first, a whole new area of experience. Eventually, she groped her way through a maze of confidences from her friends, and endless advice from Roz about "relationships," learning about people, caring about them.

Big things. She never offered much of a substantial helpful nature about the little things that came up on those initial traumatic occasions. What to do when you found you didn't really like the guy, and he wanted to kiss you an hour and a half into the first date. Or didn't want to stop there.

How you said no when you did like someone a lot, but not enough to get into a whole new dimension you weren't ready for. How you turned down a date without hurting someone's feelings.

Julie still found it hard to decide whether this kind of game-playing was rougher on a guy, ego on the line, risking rejection and not a very gentle one sometimes. Or a girl who had to wait to be asked for a date.

Of course girls didn't have to do that these days. There wasn't anything wrong with asking a guy out, but Julie felt it was something she could never do. Not that she thought anybody she liked would be apt to turn down such a bid, either. She merely found it uncomfortable even thinking about the possibility of rejection.

Her aunt never seemed to understand her feelings about something like that. She simply couldn't get the picture. Maybe because she already had an image of Julie that remained stubbornly imposed on the reality that Julie herself was unsure about.

She never told Roz that Tim Markley wasn't at all the clean-cut junior grade Robert Redford her aunt considered him. He'd been really gross, as a matter of fact, full of raunchy jokes and with a super ego, to boot. Most of the girls fell all over him, so maybe he was entitled.

Greg Horton hadn't been any prize, either, even with money to burn and a fantastic brain. He drank too much, and he got mean about driving when he'd had a couple too many. She had broken up with him a month ago, figuring that riding in that neat white Corvette was hardly worth getting mangled some day on the freeway.

Nick Devore had been fun last night, though, impressed by Roz, and agreeably astonished when she said her piece (as Julie kept wishing she wouldn't) about leaving it up to them what time they got home. A really heavy number to lay on her, she thought now, still a little cross about it. What if she hadn't liked Nick well enough to spend a half dozen hours in his company?

"Good movie?" her aunt inquired from the counter. She filled her mug from the coffee-maker, then turned in time to catch Julie's expression. "What's the matter? Oh, honey, did you have that rotten dream again? I thought you were awfully quiet this morning."

Julie made a weary gesture, lacking the energy

to lie but knowing she would end up wishing she had.

"Now don't deny it." Roz sat down to sip the fresh coffee, obviously trying to summon fresh insight on a subject well-worn from previous sessions. "Sweetie, I keep telling you it isn't healthy to repress a thing like that. A recurring dream is trying to tell you something."

She frowned. "If only we could figure out what it is. Same emotion this time? And the detail — the crash and then the search through the fog?"

"Yes."

"Whatever can it be you're looking for?"

"Maybe I'm looking for whatever it was I lost."

Her aunt didn't seem to hear the murmured words. It was just as well, Julie thought. Funny how people could throw away a line like that, casually or with a little laugh, and nobody picked up on it. You could say what you actually thought or felt, and if you didn't make a big deal of it, nobody paid any attention.

She took a deep breath, wondering how she could change the subject without being too obvious. If Roz realized how much she disliked talking about that stupid dream, they'd be here for hours, dissecting and analyzing it. Her aunt was really into dream analysis.

"It's almost nine," Julie said. "Didn't you have an appointment this morning?"

"Is it that late?" Roz hastily finished her coffee. "I'm supposed to pick up big Hal. If I can swing this condo deal, Babe, we'll have a merry merry Christmas, indeed."

She disappeared down the hall, and Julie began to load the dishwasher. As soon as she had the place cleaned up, she would go down to the Martones. She hated being alone in the house. And this morning, she seemed to have a special need for people.

Twenty minutes later, Roz poked her head in the kitchen door, still stuffing papers in the compartments of an enormous bag, the ivory tag to her key ring between her teeth.

She said around it, indistinctly, "I'm off." Then as she paused to glance around the spotless kitchen, she removed the key ring and shook her head. "All the years you've lived in this house, and you're still nasty neat. I must have failed miserably somehow. The odd couple, that's us, a clean-up freak and a total slob. Honey, you'd never believe the joys of — " She looked at the clock, winced, and blew Julie a kiss. Moments later, her small sports car growled down the long drive.

Julie grinned to herself. She didn't mind vacuuming the house or doing the laundry on Saturday mornings. A woman came in occasionally to do windows and heavy cleaning. Julie rather enjoyed the rest, the feeling of accomplishment, the satisfaction in bringing order out of the clutter Roz left in her path. Her aunt did the shopping and cooking and took care of the huge assortments of plants in the house and on the patio. It seemed a fair division of labor.

Turning on the stereo to fill the silence with music, Julie went from room to room in her usual methodical pattern, making side trips to load the washer and dryer, folding and putting away the clean clothes.

Shortly after eleven, she locked the front door and walked down the street toward Teresa's house. Her footsteps quickened as she went. By the time she turned in at the walk in front of the redwood-and-brick house on the big corner lot, she had psyched herself up, already smiling in anticipation. The moment the door opened, she'd be "on," surrounded by the warm wonderful people she loved, next to her aunt, more than anyone else in the world.

CHAPTER 2

Mrs. Martone opened the door, and her round face came alive with a sunny smile. "Farfalla!" she exclaimed, absurd delight in her voice inasmuch as she was apt to find Julie on her doorstep almost every day of the week.

From the first stages of the girls' friendship, she called her daughter's friend "Farfalla," which meant butterfly in Italian. Julie found the word enchanting. It *sounded* like a butterfly drifting on warm air currents from flower to flower.

Sometimes Mrs. Martone qualified the affectionate term, and Julie would be a laughing butterfly or a sad one. Or one suffering from a malady that sounded alarmingly sinister in Italian, but proved in loose translation to mean borderline malnutrition. Naturally, the miracles Mrs. Martone wrought with pasta were considered a happy cure for even incipient ailments.

12

Her own name was Angelina, which seemed enormously appropriate in Julie's view. She called Teresa's mother Mama Angel, a slight variation of the nickname used by the rest of the family, Angel Mama. Julie set a high value on her opinion, even though she was sure Mama Angel's image of her was nearly as wide of the mark as Aunt Roz's.

Somehow, it didn't seem to make much difference as long as Julie could be sure that kind of error stemmed from an overabundance of love. Still, it gave her a sort of sneaky feeling sometimes. She would think, yeah, she was fooling them, all right, making them see her as one kind of person when she was certain reality was something else again.

"Teresa's catching up with her mending," her mother said and gestured toward the back of the house. "Go on back, honey. She'll be glad to have company." Amusement sparkled in the dark eyes, and she added mildly, "As long as it isn't a twin brother!"

Julie grinned. Tony must be giving his sister a bad time, she thought.

On the way down the hall, she drew in a deep breath, inhaling not only the spicy cooking smells from the kitchen but also the sounds and the presence of people. Mama Martone singing while she prepared lunch. Tony mowing the lawn in back and, as the sound of the mower ceased for a moment, yelling something to his father that evoked a bellow of laughter from the garage.

13

For a moment, Julie stood in the door of her friend's room, watching Teresa. She had her mother's lovely olive skin, the same wide brown eyes, as well as Angel's even happy nature. It was the smaller version of her father's Roman nose she deplored, claiming it was fine for both Tonys, but far too much nose for a girl. Julie considered it a handsome feature, adding strength and character and interest to a face that might have settled for serenity, a gentle placid expression.

Her friend looked up abruptly as she sensed Julie's presence. "Hi," she said. "I thought you might sleep in this morning."

"No, I had to shovel out the place." Julie sat down on the floor. "How'd you like the movie?"

Her friend shrugged. "Turned out we didn't go. Couldn't find anybody to double."

It was one of Big Tony's antiquated edicts, something that always irritated Julie because such rules seemed to apply only to the girls in the family. Teresa had not been allowed to date until this year, and single dating would have to wait until her eighteenth birthday. Medieval restrictions in Julie's opinion. Yet, Teresa rarely seemed to mind as much as her friends figured she should.

"That's just the way it is," she would say in her soft voice. "Why fight it? In a few years, I'll look back and think, what difference did it make, really? They want what's best for me. They love me. That makes up for the times when they seem awfully rigid and protective."

14

Julie protested now, "Why didn't you call me?"

"And horn in on your first date with Nick?" Teresa laughed. "Not likely. Besides, it was a long movie and Nick had to work till nine, so you went to the late show, right? I would have had to go home right afterward. You didn't need that, either." She added eagerly, "Did you like him? Did you have fun?"

Julie nodded. "He's okay. Lucky, because Roz came on with the usual line about no curfews. I didn't get in till two." She held out her hand as Teresa threaded a needle and picked up a button to sew on the pink sweater in her lap. "Want me to do that?"

"Thanks. I'll be through then, as soon as I fix the rip in my blouse." A moment later, she looked up to comment, "Tony said he saw you. He didn't know you and Greg had called it quits."

Julie glanced at her, aware of the reason Tony hadn't known about that split. A confidence was always safe with Teresa. If in doubt whether an item should be considered classified information, Teresa kept her mouth shut. And there was nothing secret about the fact that Julie no longer dated Greg Horton.

"I'll bet he was happy to hear that," she said, her tone wry. "If he hadn't freaked out the minute he heard we were going together, well, I might have broken up with Greg a long time ago." She added tightly, "I wish that brother of yours would get off my case."

15

She paused then to consider the strange chemistry that existed between her and Teresa's twin. She didn't exactly bristle when he came on the scene. She merely seemed to brace herself. Because Tony persisted in judging her. If he didn't come right out and put his disapproval into words, it was obvious in the set of his mouth and the expression in his unsmiling dark eyes. He was Big Tony's son, for sure, protective and watchful of the women in the family, an attitude that sometimes extended to his sister's friend. One who might conceivably prove a corrupting influence, Julie thought with a familiar prickle of annoyance.

"He just worries about you," Teresa said, ever the peacemaker when it seemed that trouble might be imminent. At the same time, with the ease of long practice, she managed to keep her loyalties separate and intact.

"Sure." Julie relaxed, the momentary irritation draining away. She reached for the scissors and snipped the thread. "Okay, you got all your buttons again." She gave Teresa a faint smile. "Did you practice your song for Monday?"

The other girl flushed and laughed as she shook her head. "I can't do it. Julie, I get sick to my stomach when I even think about getting up in front of all those people. I decided if something like that isn't fun, it's just really dumb to put myself through it."

"You've got a fantastic voice," Julie insisted. "When you have a gift like that, it's even more dumb not to use it, to share it. Isn't it?"

"Nope. Not when you're talking about sharing it with the whole school. It's different with you. Something like Talent Day, that's for people who enjoy what they do. And you're so good, I can understand why you get a kick out of it." Teresa's eyes sparkled. "Have you got your sketches figured out?"

"I think so. Want to see?"

"Sure. Close the door, why don't you?"

Julie scrambled to her feet to obey. Then she grabbed a ruler from Teresa's desk to use as a mike. "They'll introduce me as Carol Burnett. I start off by explaining why I gave up my former show."

She stood by the wall, revolving slowly, mentally ticking off the three things she used in this part of a performance, aside from the voice. No one, not even Teresa, knew how much work went into these impressions. Julie studied the stars with great care, memorizing the way they held their heads, their gestures, the spacing and emphasis of their words as well as the tone of voice.

The trick was to make it look easy, as ballet dancers and skaters did. That was the magical part. Besides, people respected a skill more if someone made it look effortless. A talented person seemed more interesting, more colorful, more to be envied in that case.

Before she said a word, Julie could tell from Teresa's grin that the impression was working. "Welcome to the show." She let her smile broaden, suggesting an overbite by the set of her jaw. "I guess I owe you some kind of explanation. I mean, there were hundreds of letters asking why I gave up my show."

A slow turn of her head, eyes rolling comically as if she regretted bringing the matter up. "Actually, it was that business with my earlobe. Tugging it so often." A brief pause. "And one day, it started to grow." She gave a quick flick of her left wrist as if she were tossing a long dangling object over her shoulder.

Teresa burst out laughing.

"So, anyway, here I am to interview some mystery guests, three of my dearest friends. And the first question — I have it here someplace — " (Frantic fumbling up sleeves and in pockets before she finally located the invisible script in her shoe.) "Yes. The question for Mystery Guest Number One — what makes you happy?"

One step to the right, a different posture, head and shoulders back, the smile a bit self-conscious. "*Diamonds*, dahling! Oh, no, I don't wear zem in the daytime. Never more than six or seven — too many diamonds before noon, dahling, that's *tarrably* vulgar — !"

In a split second, Julie turned her head, widened her eyes, and stretched her mouth in an enormous happy grin. Her voice emerged in a much deeper tone, full of laughter. "Oh, that's so *silly*, Zsa! They're a girl's best friend, you know. And it's perfectly *marvelous* recreation, cleaning them, sorting them, counting them." A thoughtful pause, then in an innocent wondering tone, "If you have more than a dozen, that's just fantastically *educational* too — "

Again, Julie shifted her head, and her body moved briefly in the frantic frenzied routine Charo had made popular. One hand tossed an invisible mane of hair back from her face. The voice that spoke this time had a different inflection, a foreign flavor in the firm staccato speech.

"No, Carol, you mistake."

Carol Burnett returned, script in hand. "Then, this theory about diamonds — you feel it's a fallacy?"

"Hah?" said Charo.

"A fallacy. Do you think these ladies are wrong?"

"Chass. Absolutely. Switty, anybody ever tell you you talk fonny?"

Teresa giggled. Then her head jerked toward the door as someone rapped softly.

Tony stuck his head around it. For a moment, he looked from one girl to the other, a smile forming as he studied their startled faces. His eyes were darker than Teresa's, under thick brows, like straight black strokes from a painter's brush. Short, shaggy curls glistened now as if he'd run wet hands through them.

"Thought I'd catch your act," he said to Julie. "Are you through with the first show?"

She grinned at him. "Nose trouble?" she inquired in a long-running joke between them. "You should have sent it on ahead."

"Nah. I woulda missed the whole thing. It always gets there five minutes before I do." He leaned against the door frame. "Come on, give me a preview, Jule. I can't wait till Monday."

She stared at him. Then she brought her hands up in a boxer's stance and recited in the hoarse familiar singsong of Muhammad Ali:

> That Martone, he's pretty scary
> His secret weapon's really hairy
> I soon found out this honky cat
> Had a nose that knocked me flat.

Tony laughed. "*That's* cool. But you gotta admit, it's the only thing that saves me from being just another pretty face."

"Me too," Teresa said dolefully.

Julie regarded them with affectionate exasperation. "*Really*," she said. "I can see it now, the hassle you'll both have to find work. Only an occasional house-haunting fee to keep body and soul together. Tough."

Tony folded his arms across his chest, looking at her indulgently down the nose she thought so splendid. And would have died before she told him so. "We can always count on you for good references," he said in a slow lazy voice, "when you're really big in show biz."

"Reminds me," she said, serious now. "What've you heard about Mr. Lawton?"

He shrugged. "No mystery. Just what you read in the *Star-News*. He chucked a 'promising career as an actor' to teach drama and history at M.V. High. The theater's loss, our gain."

"But why?" she persisted. "Why would anyone come to a place like this, way back in the boonies — deliberately?"

"Way I hear it, because he has a retarded child. The school here has something special to offer."

"Oh," Teresa said on a sad note. "What a neat thing for him to do."

Tony was still watching Julie, a speculative expression in his eyes. "He's a pro," he said softly. "I think if I were you, I'd get my act together before next semester. That class won't be a snap, even if you're loaded with talent. The guy's going to be really heavy on discipline."

She glared at him. "You never miss a chance for the needle, do you? Listen, if I wanted advice, I'd write to Dear Abby."

Amusement flickered across his face. "In your case, why don't you make it Dial-a-Prayer?"

Teresa got to her feet. "Come on, you guys — "

But it was Big Tony's shouted summons that snapped the tension.

"Everybody to the table!" he thundered from the other end of the hall. "When all the chairs are full, we lock the door! Last call for lunch!"

CHAPTER 3

Julie leaned against her locker, watching the kids stream by along the corridor as she waited for Nick. When he appeared, he'd be loping along on the fringes, not looking as if he were in any special hurry to get where he was going. With the length of his stride, however, he could cover a lot of distance in a very short time. Before she knew him well, she had been surprised by his grace in various sports.

Last Friday night, she made another discovery. Those enormous hands capable of handling a basketball with startling ease had cradled her face with a gentle, tentative touch. It was as if he had learned to be wary of his strength, controlling the power in his tall, sparsely fleshed body.

Julie had been oddly moved by the sudden flash of insight. As a rule, she was not adept at

22

sizing people up. Her rare moments of perception warmed her, therefore, with extraordinary satisfaction.

Now she glanced at her watch and thought a bit uneasily, Nick had better not be late today. They were due at the gym for the tryouts in less than ten minutes. Teresa wouldn't be able to save space for them for long in the front row of the bleachers.

She saw him then, dodging around a group of girls, grinning over his shoulder as one of them playfully grabbed his arm. A moment later, he skidded to a halt, fingers plowing through his light brown hair. The blue eyes that were always full of laughter softened as he looked down at her.

Julie smiled at him, feeling again a warm buoyancy inside. It was an instant reflection of the message in those eyes, that she was his girl, unique, distinctive, without flaw.

"Sorry I'm late," he said. His slow voice still bore traces of a southern accent, though he had lived in California since he was nine. "History test." He winced. "A wipeout."

As they hurried down the outer corridor, she punched his arm lightly and felt the muscles contract, solid as a brick under her knuckles. She played it for laughs, recoiling as if she'd broken her hand, leaving it in midair for several seconds, dangling limp from the wrist.

"I'm damaged," she said owlishly. Then, in a quicksilver change, she laughed. "A wipeout? The way you study, Nicko, not likely."

"Thanks."

He took her hand and swung it, holding it with that curiously gentle grip. She couldn't be sure yet whether it meant more than the apprehension she had sensed about the strength in his big hands. Then again it might be his way of letting her direct certain things about their relationship at this initial stage. Possibly, he was telling her without putting it in words, "I like to touch you, but if you'd rather not be touched right now, just take your hand away."

A far cry from Greg who had assumed too much, an amiable bully at the beginning, then merely a bully. He loved to argue, usually about some dumb thing like whether you could put Barry Manilow in the same category as Peter Frampton. Julie would think, irritated, who said you had to put them together? He could be a real drag about something like that, bringing out the worst in her with alarming ease.

She found herself needling him constantly or baiting him. "You're always trying to compare things like apples and oranges or cats and dogs," she'd say loftily. "Anything for a really heavy *discussion*. I know where you're coming from, Gregoravitch. Macho country. I always have to agree with you — or I'm being hostile. Right?"

By that time, naturally, she was oozing hostility from every pore. Underneath the pressure of dark emotion, she felt a curious excitement, even a faint spark of pleasure when she saw the flush of anger on his face.

"Macho," she repeated with emphasis.

"Spelled backwards, that's ohcam. And that's the way you'd spell it, Charlie. Because your brain's so fat, you've got the worst cholesterol problem known to medical science. From the ears up, that is."

It ended in a huge fight, of course. It always did. Why did she inevitably break up with a guy in a blood-and-thunder battle? She told herself bitterly, she had a class act going, for sure.

She still felt uncomfortable about that last unpleasant scene, though Roz had tried to soothe her the next morning.

"It's the only way to go," she had said firmly. "Honey, the woods are full of turkeys like that. So you spelled it out for him. Maybe you did him a favor. If he didn't get the message this time, he'll get a rerun from the next girl he tries that number on. Psychological karate, that's what it is. Who needs it?"

No, it hadn't helped much. Because every time Julie tried to tell herself her aunt was right, she would think about Roz's wretched track record. She meant well, but she just didn't carry much weight as an authority about men.

Now, as Nick reached for the latch to the big double doors in front of the gym, Julie grabbed his arm. "Nick," she said in a soft urgent voice.

He paused and looked at her, curious.

"I just want you to know something," she said and felt her face burn with unaccustomed shyness. "I just want you to know — I'll never do anything — intentionally — to hurt you."

He bent to her, his lips firm on hers for a

moment. "I'll never hurt you, either, Julie. Quit worrying about us. We go together like — like grits and gravy. You'll see, we're gonna be just fine."

Seconds later, through the big doors, the first person she saw was Greg Horton. He turned away quickly, his face stiff, and Julie felt her smile fade, the sting of tears behind her eyes.

It seemed like an ugly omen. Because several months ago, she and Greg had made promises to each other too, all of them broken rather violently in the heat of their final battle. Only the acid memory remained, burning across her mind.

Julie saw Teresa waving frantically from the next section of bleachers, and they made their way over to her.

"Thank goodness," Teresa said with a groan. "I couldn't have saved your seats for another minute. Hi, Nick, are you going to try out too?"

He laughed. "Not unless they're desperate for a retired yo-yo champ."

He turned with the others as the volume of noise abruptly dipped to a subdued murmur. A slight, thin-faced man strode to the microphone set up at the far end of the gym. He looked at the crowd for a moment, unhurried, head turning as he seemed to study each individual face.

Julie stared at him. She wasn't quite sure what she had expected of Craig Lawton, the New York actor who had turned his back on a "promising career" to teach at Mesa Verde High. But she felt a faint disappointment in the flesh-and-blood reality after all the intriguing rumors. This man with the nondescript face and thinning gray-blonde hair looked more like an accountant or a clerk in a department store. Someone who might sell shoes or men's clothing at the local Sears.

Then the microphone made a sharp crackling sound, and Mr. Lawton said into it, "Good afternoon, ladies and gentlemen." A ripple of laughter. Someone in the rear whistled shrilly. "Welcome to the Talent Day tryouts. You are about to witness or experience an event similar to one known in the theater as a cattle call."

He held up one hand, and a smile lit the narrow bony face. "Don't let the callous term disturb you. That sated sardonic creature called a director on Broadway would be judging you with a world-wearied eye, hoping you might have something he could use, something which might help him. I'm here, on the other hand, to look for something I might be able to help you develop." A sweeping graceful gesture included the entire audience, quiet now, giving him their complete attention.

"That's it," he said crisply. "You already know the procedure. We'll take you alphabetically. Step to the mike, give your name and a brief description of your routine. The key word, people, is brief. We have until five o'clock, and that's going to limit us unless you make it short and snappy. So, if you're a singer, step up and say loud and clear, 'Singer.' Then sing. Let your talent speak for you. First on the roster, Roberta Ames. Go, Roberta."

As he stepped back from the microphone, Julie let out the breath she had held during most of his speech. Magic, she thought. Pure magic. The moment he began to speak, the image of a bland, mild-mannered salesman vanished, and he became the most interesting person in the crowded gym. His voice was musical, flexible, deep. She was sure it would have filled the vast barnlike building, had he cared to switch off the mike.

Presence, she thought. He had that mysterious endlessly fascinating quality too. Stars in all fields had presence, even some politicians, the ones who were called statesmen, eventually. She felt excitement build within until she shivered with the prickling of goose flesh on her arms.

In that moment, she wanted desperately to know what this man must have learned long ago, how to become another person at will. People like Mr. Lawton certainly didn't suffer image problems. He had to know exactly who he was and why. He had learned somehow to tap an inner power. He must know some kind of secret, surely the most fantastic secret in the world. She ached with a sudden yearning to discover what it might be.

With an effort, she brought her attention back to the final notes of the Judy Collins song, one rendered in a small but fiercely controlled soprano. Roberta sat down in a wave of applause, her cheeks pink.

The Albertson brothers followed her with a

medley for guitar and bass. By the time four more singers and a tumbling act had performed, Julie felt a familiar hollow sensation in her stomach. They were almost through the D's, she thought, grateful once more that her name was Enright. She could see poor Pat Zabrowski three seats away, hands clenched into white-knuckled fists on her knees. In Pat's place, Julie thought with compassion, she might self-destruct long before they called on her.

"Enright!"

Nick squeezed her hand and wished her luck as she got to her feet and ran to the mike. "Julie Enright," she said a little breathlessly. "Impressions."

By the time she launched into Carol Burnett, she knew it was going well. Her nerves were calm again, serving merely to put an edge on her performance. She was always better in front of an audience, keyed to their response, responding in turn to laughter, to an individual face watching intently, to the hush that followed each burst of amusement. Though she was acutely conscious of Mr. Lawton standing at the left, just out of her range of vision, she didn't look at him until she was almost through, midway in Charo's dialogue.

He was laughing.

Adrenelin surging, Julie went back to her seat through a roar of applause, riding the wave of sound, the warmth and approval that surrounded her, almost a tangible thing. Just before she reached her place, one of the girls yelled to her through the dwindling uproar, "Hey! Do Miz Gorilla!"

Impulsively, Julie obeyed. Hunching her shoulders, she strode the last few feet, lower lip extended in a brutal caricature of Miss Varilla, the P.E. teacher. "Once around the track, ladies," she rasped in a practiced parody of the teacher's husky voice. "Come on, ladies, let's get the lead out."

Laughter erupted once more from the kids in the nearby rows who had heard her. Farther down the line and across the gym, heads turned and a puzzled buzz went through the ranks as people sought the source of the brief hilarity.

Julie sat down between Teresa and Nick, who was still laughing. Her friend's smile looked a little strained, though she clutched her arm and murmured, "Great! Really great!"

Nick said in her ear, "You are far *out*, you know it?"

"Shhh!" someone hissed behind them.

There was no chance to talk further. Nick had to leave before five to get to his job at a discount store a few blocks away.

When the tryouts ended, Julie sat with Teresa, waiting for the crowd to clear out ahead of them. Already, she felt herself coming down from the great natural high she always experienced in front of an audience.

"Teresa? Hey, tell me the truth. Was the thing on Miz Gorilla — ?" She made a face. "Was it — too much, maybe?"

"Uh —" Teresa hesitated, distress in her dark eyes. "I know you didn't see her, but she was back there by the door. Watching."

"Oh, wow." Julie clutched her head.

"Just a matter of — bad timing. It wasn't as if —"

Tony appeared behind his sister, hands on her shoulders, so she stopped and looked up at him. Unsmiling, he stared at Julie for a moment. "What it was," he said in a voice edged with scorn, "was a cheap shot. That's what it *was*, Jule Baby."

She lifted her chin. "Did I ask you?"

He grinned. "Nope. Figured it must be an oversight. Rest of your act? Dynamite."

"Thanks," she said coolly.

Tony laughed. "I mean it, for what it's worth. And believe me, knowing you, I've got a good idea what it's worth."

Teresa stirred uneasily.

But before Julie could come up with a suitably stinging retort, she saw the twins glance over her shoulder. She turned to see Mr. Lawton approaching. Her heart gave a little jerk as she realized his faint smile was directed at her.

"Enright? See you a minute?"

Julie gulped. "Me? Oh — sure."

Following him to one side, she waited as he studied her for several endless seconds. Her heart was hammering now like a wild thing beating against her ribs.

"Enright," he said again. The deep powerful voice at close range sent shivers up her spine.

"You're not in my class." The clear gray eyes watched her quizzically.

After a moment, she realized it had been a question, and felt herself flush. "Uh — no," she said. "Next semester. I mean I hope you'll — I can't take it until next — "

His head moved briefly. "Any formal training?"

She had begun to recognize the abbreviated pattern of his speech. "No. No, but I hope — "

Again the brief movement of his head cut her off. Clearly, it was his version of a nod.

"Good. There's considerable — potential." He stared at her, head back, his eyes narrowed, speculative. "Would you like to sit in on some of the sessions after school? We'll be casting the first play. No chance for you to do much. Just observe. How do you — ?"

"Oh, I'd love it. Yes, I'd really — "

"Good." He turned away, then glanced back at her. "I want to make one thing clear. Keep up the work in your other classes. If this interferes, if your grades slip — even one C and you're out. Understood?"

"Yes."

He gave her his quick appealing smile. "Great. You've got talent, Julie. Is there discipline to go with it?"

"Oh, I — I — "

"You don't know yet," he said firmly. "Neither do I. But I can tell you one thing for sure. We'll find out in a hurry. Okay?"

"Yes. Okay."

Bursting with excitement, she went back to the twins to blurt out the news of the wonderful, incredible invitation Mr. Lawton had extended.

Teresa hugged her happily.

Even Tony grinned and thumped her on the back the way he did on the rare occasions when he was pleased with her. But being Tony, he couldn't resist another half pound of advice.

"If you want to make points with that one, honey, you better shape up fast."

Julie flared, anger roughening her voice. "Will you get off my back, Tony? You never miss an opportunity — "

"You're the one who never does that," he said soberly. "The easy laugh. You go for it every time. Listen, you don't play games with Golden Boy. If he'd caught your number on Miz Gorilla, you would have cooked your chances to get in his class next semester. Let alone — "

But Julie whirled and headed for the door. Maybe Teresa put up with that garbage, but she sure didn't have to stand still for it. She thought furiously, if she stayed around, she'd end up telling him to shut that big mouth of his. He had spoiled all her good feeling about what the drama teacher had said, dimming the glow before she'd had two minutes to enjoy it.

As if she didn't know she'd have to be careful around Mr. Lawton. Nobody had to spell that out for her. She had never met anybody like him. And certainly she had never felt such a feverish need before to impress another person. She would do almost anything to learn his secret.

33

She thought about that all the way home, a sense of wonder gradually replacing the residue of anger. She would be the best student Mr. Lawton had ever had, she told herself, the most dedicated, the most cooperative. And she'd begin by being a mouse-quiet, alert observer. It would be the most important project in her life, figuring out what went on behind those thoughtful gray eyes. But first, she had to win Mr. Lawton's approval.

CHAPTER 4

Roz had called to say she might be late, but she would bring pizza for dinner. She breezed in a few minutes after seven just as Julie finished making the salad. Still in a dark mood over Tony's remarks in the gym, she welcomed the distraction her aunt provided.

Roz always replayed the events of the day with her own verbal punctuation. She would add a growled aside as she identified the various players in a particular incident, then give a brief scream of laughter when she reached the denouement. No one could deliver a punchline with better timing, emphasizing her point with scathing scorn or outrageous wit, whichever the story seemed to demand.

Tonight, she sat across the table from her niece, brown eyes shining as she nibbled daintily at a slice of pizza. Her sleeveless white silk blouse contrasted dramatically with the tan acquired during hours on the tennis court. After a few minutes, however, she glanced at Julie and her quick light voice cut off in mid-sentence.

She raised her wine glass and sipped the dark red liquid, studying her niece thoughtfully. "Sure you wouldn't like some wine?"

Julie made a face. "It's that sour stuff. No thanks."

Her aunt shrugged. "Grows on you. I keep telling you, you have to develop a taste for some things. Dry wine, ripe olives, caviar, anchovies." She sighed. "And some people."

Julie smiled faintly and commented in her quavering little-old-lady voice, "So if at first you don't succeed —"

"You got it." Roz nodded. "People who have taste don't need a thing to go with it. Oh, a little money, maybe, and enough looks to get by —"

Julie didn't hear the rest, still hung up on a word in the first part of that absurd solemn speech. *Taste*, she thought. When a person had good taste, they didn't go for the easy laugh, the cheap shots that were always good for — And there she was, back again to the scene in the gym, to Tony looking at her with disapproval in the cool dark eyes. *"That's what it was, Jule Babe . . . . You don't play games with Golden Boy. . . ."*

She felt the slow simmer of anger once more. People who were invariably right could be crashing bores. C.B.'s she called them. And in her book, Anthony Martone was Super C.B., himself.

She looked up to see her aunt shaking her head.

One slim hand brushed at the slant of black bangs, an habitual unconscious gesture. "Are you back?" she asked gently. Then her eyes widened. "But today was — I never thought to ask about the tryouts. Is that why you're — ? Don't tell me they didn't *like* what you did?"

With a supreme effort, Julie put light amusement in her voice. "Are you crazy? They've got superb taste at M.V. And Mr. Lawton's fantastic. He asked me to sit in on the sessions after school."

"Oh, honey, that's great. What did Nick say about your sketches?"

Julie laughed. In the prim voice of Lily Tomlin's character, Mrs. Earbore, she said, "He thought it was *tasteful*, the most *tasteful* thing he's ever seen." She changed tone, sober now. "Nicko — I really like him."

"Still waters," said Roz obscurely. "The quiet ones, they grow on you, all right." She helped herself to more salad and said to the piece of lettuce on her fork, "Maybe it's time you made an appointment with Dr. Wiegand."

Julie's head jerked up. Then she released the quick breath in a noisy sigh that puffed past her lips. "Just because I said I like him — "

"Julie, I can't read you lately. I honestly can't figure out where you're at." Bright color glowed across her aunt's cheekbones. "Every time I mention sensible precautions, you do this virtuous-maiden number on me." She spaced her words

37

carefully, her voice crisp. "We are living in new enlightened times. This is not 1880. So I feel very strongly that — "

"I know how you feel! You've spelled it out enough times. I wish you'd quit pushing!" The tears that had been close to the surface ever since she got home evaporated in the heat of her anger. It flashed now through the flood of words she knew she would regret. Yet the knowledge was a flimsy barrier against the tide of strong emotion.

"Open season on Enright! Let's get everybody into the act till the kid shapes up. I'd like to know how you can all be so damned sure you're right about what kind of person I am — or should be — when *I* don't have the faintest clue."

Her aunt's head snapped back as if Julie had lashed out at her physically, slapping her across the face. The dark eyes were bright, almost as if they held unshed tears. "That's not fair," she said softly. "If you're unsure about yourself, Julie, it's something everyone goes through at your age. The one thing I've always wanted you to know is that I'm here to help, to stand behind you."

"You don't understand! I think it's great that you — I *know* you love me. You want me to be happy. So I feel really rotten when I yell at you." She struggled to lower her voice, ragged now, straining past the lump in her throat. "But, Aunt Roz, you can't seem to understand that —

that it doesn't help when you — you just tell me I can do anything I want to do."

Roz gave a short laugh. When she spoke, it was more in puzzled sorrow than in anger. "I hardly think I've gone that far, giving you carte blanche to — look, I just want to spare you the frustration and fury that practically ate me up in my growing years. All the stupid rigid rules that made no sense. Let me tell you, it wasn't any picnic. So I have to ask, what do you *want* from me?"

She flung out thin lovely hands in a gesture that echoed the baffled note in her voice. "Do you *want* rules and regulations? Do you *want* a silly curfew? So you can break it the very first time you're out having fun and you don't feel like coming home at the hour we set? Is that what you want?"

They had gone over the same ground so many times, the lines settled into familiar patterns. More than once, Roz had promised faithfully that she would set a curfew if Julie felt more comfortable with one.

But by the time her date appeared that evening or a week later, her aunt inevitably would have forgotten the discussion. Or she would say the next morning, "He was so gorgeous, honey, I figured you'd want me to let you off the hook. Midnight's a ridiculous hour to come home from a dance."

Besides, Roz seemed to be equating the really heavy stuff about sex with a trivial matter like a curfew. It added to the turmoil of confusion that led in turn to Julie's occasional flash of anger.

She pushed a slice of mushroom around her plate, impaling it at last rather violently with one tine of her fork. "Let's just — forget it, okay? I'm sorry I yelled and hollered at you. Only — I wish you'd quit harping on the doctor thing."

She looked up, her eyes burning. Her voice sounded as tired as she felt. "Look, every single girl I know who's into sex, they're even more mixed-up than I am. That's the last thing I need. More problems."

"All right." Roz frowned. "I can't figure it, you know? Anybody with all you've got going for you — brains, talent, looks — "

"But not much taste," Julie said, surprised herself at the bitterness in her voice. "As for looks — Aunt Roz, when I meet a girl and I think she's fantastically beautiful and then I find out she's mean or selfish or she tells lies all the time — I end up wondering why I ever thought she was pretty. And it works the other way too. Somebody can come along looking like Dracula's sister, and then I find out she's so *great*, I never see the homely things about her anymore."

Her aunt leaned forward, her eyes curious. "So? How do you think people see you, Julie?"

"I don't know." She stared at the mushroom slice, brought it slowly to her mouth and bit into it. "How do I know how they see me when *I* can't see me?"

"What do you mean? When you look in a

mirror, you see a remarkably pretty girl. Don't you?"

Julie looked at her. "No," she said. "I don't think I'm pretty. Besides, when I look in a mirror, I look at my hair — and comb it. Or at my eyes when I'm putting makeup on. Or at my teeth if I'm brushing them."

Roz gave a whoop of laughter. "There isn't a thing wrong with you that a little mileage won't fix. I'd give an arm and a leg for that nice young skin of yours and eyelashes so long, people think they're fake." She got up and took her dishes to the kitchen, leaning across the breakfast bar to add, "Take my word for it, sweetie, when you do get it all added up, the sum total's going to boggle your mind."

"Sure." Julie sighed as she finished clearing the table. A great comfort that was. She already had the most boggled mind in Mesa Verde and possibly for fifty miles in every direction.

Minutes later, her aunt reappeared from the bedroom, lipstick repaired, a black briefcase under her arm. "I'll be late," she said. "Want to ask Teresa to spend the night?"

"No. I've got homework you wouldn't believe."

"Then lock all the doors. And don't open up to answer the doorbell until you look through the peephole and see who it is. Promise?"

"Yes, ma'am. Why don't we get a dog, Aunt Roz? A lovely big one to chew on burglars."

Her aunt laughed. "With our luck, we'd get

41

a pooch so neurotic he'd chew on the mailman, the meter readers, and all children under the age of eight."

She paused, grinning, to enlarge on that. "Burglars would have a really tough time getting the swag in a bag. Depend on it, any hound of ours would be licking the crook's hands and feet, then rolling over to have his tummy scratched."

As the door closed behind her, Julie's smile faded. It would be so neat, having a dog to keep her company when Roz went out. Between husbands, her aunt was feverishly social, and jobs in real estate meant lots of meetings and late appointments.

But Roz, who could deny Julie nothing else, balked at the idea of a pet in the household. She insisted they carried germs, and she couldn't bear the idea of cat or dog hair all over the furniture.

Unreal, Julie thought with mingled affection and annoyance, the opinion coming as it did from the slob of the universe. She might have pursued the matter and won her own way. She could almost always coax Roz into giving her something she really wanted. But her aunt once made a casual comment that Julie never forgot.

"Pets can make strange attachments," Roz had said. "I remember your mother had a big orange cat when we were little." She shuddered faintly. "What a loser he was. And you might know, he decided he loved me best of all. Broke Ann's heart. Neither of us mourned overlong the day old Oscar crossed the street in a lot of traffic — and turned in his dinner dish on the way."

Remembering, Julie made a face as she stacked the last plate in the dishwasher. It would be a horribly painful thing to have a little kitten or puppy and come to realize, after you had grown to love it dearly, that it liked someone else better.

She locked the doors, and turned out all the lights but a dim one in the hall. Back in her room, she glanced at her mother's picture, curiously comforted by the warm gray eyes so like her own, that returned her smile.

"Poor Mom," she said aloud. "He was just a no-class cat, that's all."

Then on impulse, she flopped on the bed, pillows propped behind her against the wall, and addressed the pictures of her parents.

"Well, folks, there's good news and bad news tonight. Listen, the tryout thing turned out fine. And I met Mr. Lawton. I get to sit in on all the afterschool stuff while they're reading for the first play. That part's really cool, right?"

She kicked off her sandals and swung her legs up, studying her bare toes for a moment, soberly. "Yeah, you already guessed the rest of it. Mr. Bad News Martone. Remember the time I wore my T-shirt that says 'Handle With Care' on it, and he wouldn't take us to school till I went home and changed? I swear, it wasn't so much that *he* felt uptight about it. He just didn't want me contaminating that dumb car of his. Is that freaky enough for you? We wipe our *feet* before we get in old Tony's Toyota."

Silence.

She sighed loudly. If only Nick didn't have to work until nine, she thought. If only the phone would ring. She didn't feel like studying tonight. She was much too restless, her nerves on edge as if she were still trying to sort the events of the day and figure out how they tipped the scale.

Ah, well, when in doubt, work it out. She got off the bed and went to scrub down the walls of her shower. Then she scrubbed herself and made a mug of hot tea to drink while she did her nails, an old Beatles album on the stereo. After that, she ran through the sketches for Talent Day, studying herself in the full-length mirror on her closet door.

Shortly after eleven, she turned out the light and smiled as she glanced at the shadowy outlines of the pictures on the what-not shelf. In her mind, she said to them softly, "You would have made me do my homework, wouldn't you?"

CHAPTER 5

The next morning she found Teresa waiting for her at the curb in front of the Martone home.

"I wanted to call you last night," her friend said, "but my father was on the phone till almost ten. And I can't make any calls after that."

Julie sighed. "I know. It's okay. I wasn't mad at *you*."

"Well, I thought I'd catch you this morning," Teresa said, "to tell you something so you'll understand. If Tony comes on pretty strong, and I guess he does, it's the thing with Dad again. Really heavy."

Julie glanced toward the house and saw the Toyota in the drive, but there was no sign of Tony. "Yeah," she said, "it's a regular epidemic. I went a couple rounds with my aunt last night. Might as well have given it to her in Afghanistan — is there a language like that?"

"I don't know. Probably."

"Anyway, I'm *trying* to get through." Julie lifted one shoulder, easing the weight of the books in her arms. "I still think if Tony just sat down with your dad and said, 'Look, I don't want any part of the contracting business, I want to major in psychology —'"

"He told him that last night." Teresa nodded as she saw the surprise on Julie's face. "He came right out with it, said he wanted to work with kids, the ones in trouble or disturbed or handicapped or —"

"What did your dad say?"

Teresa winced. "In a way, I guess it would have been better if he'd stomped around and made a lot of noise about it. At least Tony would know he'd made a point, that Dad was taking him seriously, even if he didn't go along with it."

"Well, what did he *say*?"

"He said Tony'd outgrow the notion — that's what he called it, a notion — just like he got over wanting to be a policeman or a fireman or an astronaut. He *laughed*." Teresa's low voice held a note of pain. "He did everything but pat Tony on the head. Oh, Julie, I was so scared he'd do something like that. Because Tony had that awful look — Mom calls it his Sicilian gangster look — and it always means he's right on the edge, about to lose control."

"He didn't — ?"

"No, thank goodness. He got up and slammed out of the house. Mom said he didn't get in till almost midnight."

"What did she do?"

Teresa shook her head sadly. "Talked to Dad, I suppose. She looked really beat this morning. But this isn't one of those things she's going to fix just by talking. Both Dad and Tony are so stubborn, and she's in the middle, of course. Like I am."

At the sound of a door slamming, she touched Julie's arm. "Go easy, huh? I know he gets pretty impossible. He's just like Dad. But it's only because he feels as if — well, you're like one of his sisters."

Julie shuddered and said in her Paul Lynde voice, "What a revolting idea!" But she gave Tony her sunniest smile as she crawled into the back seat of his car. "*Good* morning, Anthony. You're wearing those terrific jeans again. And you shaved your nose and forehead. Law! Ah think ahm in luuuuuv!"

Tony struggled briefly against a tight smile. Settled behind the wheel, he tossed a mimeographed sheet over his shoulder. "Listen, you two, make yourselves useful. With my luck, I'll get a vocabulary quiz first thing today. Test me, will you?" He glanced at them as he backed out. "Teresa? You better do it. Greta Gargle's got a bad case of the cutes today."

Julie giggled, but she contented herself during the short ride by listing silently the things she might have said. After all, Tony never let a chance go by to take a shot at her about her grades.

"Underachiever of the year," he would say

with a grin. "It's not the smarts you have that count, Juliet, it's the smarts you use."

And she'd retort instantly in Sweet Southern, "Oh, land, Big Daddy, how evah did ah live through a single day befoah you came down the road? Ah just admiah the way you he'p and as*sist* me with youah luhvly pro*found* re*mocks*."

Today she pressed her lips together, feeling virtuous, and listened as Teresa ran her twin through the Spanish vocabulary list. As she got out of the car, he ruffled his sister's short black curls. "Thanks," he said.

Then he looked over the hood at Julie who had scrambled out the other side. "Hey," he said, "I want you to know I don't shave my nose for just anybody. I got this flash you were going to wear pink today." He gave her a dazzling smile. "Honey, if you go pink from now till the day we vote, you're a shoo-in for Homecoming Princess."

Julie laughed, but she felt her cheeks burn with the same color as her outfit. Every time she settled into a good satisfying phase, turning Tony off no matter what he said, she could depend on him coming on like Mister Charm. Sometimes she wondered if he did it deliberately, taking an evil delight in keeping her off balance.

Still in her pensive subdued mood, she found Nick waiting by her locker and greeted him without enthusiasm.

"Julie, I wanted to call last night," he said and paused, looking a bit uneasy as he watched her sorting through her books.

"So why didn't you?"

He shifted his weight to the other foot and aimed a gentle kick at the lower row of lockers. "Vocabulary quiz today," he said and groaned. "Plus a mountain of homework. I figured if I got off work early, I could handle it and still have time to — but I didn't get home till 9:30."

Julie looked at him over her shoulder. She would have given a lot for a phone call last night. It had been the pits, for sure, that scene in the gym, then the depressing session at dinner. She could have used somebody to unload on at that point, even by way of Ma Bell. Still, she dumped on Teresa too often as it was. Why start that with Nick? People got sick of the soggy shoulder routine after a while, even nice guys like Nick Devore.

Her aunt had said once in her clear light voice, "Men will put up with a lot, but a moody lady drives them up the wall."

Julie suspected she was right about that. But it seemed to her that Roz lost interest in pleasing or trying to impress a man the minute she married him. Maybe when it came down to it, her aunt didn't really like men. Julie put the curious idea aside for future examination.

"One of us has to be practical and sensible," she said demurely and batted her lashes at Nick. "Obviously, we're going to be a smashing success as a team. You'll be the clever one, and I'll add the class."

He grinned, looking relieved. "Way to go," he

said and fell into step beside her as she hurried down the corridor.

She managed to finish her English assignment during the reading of the bulletin and the announcements in Advisory, luckily a lengthy affair today. She didn't have the biology terms memorized as Miss Coleman had requested, but she figured she wouldn't have to sweat that until the next test.

The teacher was a tall skinny woman, who wore Ben Franklin glasses on her thin elegant nose, crisp graying hair in perpetual disarray. She had a habit of pawing through it at intervals, long fingers clutching her head. It was as if she figured judicious application of pressure might stimulate her thought processes.

Early in the year, Julie discovered that it was easy to divert Miss Coleman from class routine when she found something amusing. The teacher invariably dissolved in helpless laughter when Julie went to work on her. A class like biology offered a wealth of material, though the humor inherent in the subject could be pretty gross at times.

When she came through the door to the lab, two girls at the front desk called to her. "Julie, did you see the movie Friday?"

She dumped her books on her stool. "Yeah. It was okay. I mean, Henry Winkler's *fantastic*, but the movie — " She flipped one hand in a gesture indicating a marginal opinion. "My first date with Nick," she said and laughed. "By the time we finished talking about the show — "

Cindy groaned. A plump girl with dull blonde hair that nearly reached her waist, she had just begun to date this year. "You didn't get home till three, I bet," she cut in. "Man, if I'm in one minute after midnight — sometimes eleven o'clock — I'm grounded for a week."

Betty Jo tucked a pencil behind her ear and stared at Julie with small, deep-set blue eyes. "And you don't even have to baby-sit. Wow. If I got a decent allowance, you can bet I wouldn't, either. Every Saturday night, four hours with the Hansen brats. Slave wages at that."

Julie made sympathetic noises. Poor Betty Jo had a face that would warp the insides of any clock around. It wasn't any wonder that she didn't date. Besides, the two girls were inseparable. The surprising thing was that any guy had found Cindy alone long enough to get acquainted.

"You don't know how lucky you are," she said. Hooking her thumbs beneath her heavy hair, she pulled it back off her shoulders. "Your aunt's so neat. I saw her the other day in that terrific little car. It isn't any wonder she's been married — " She broke off, round face flushing.

"Three times," Julie said coolly. "Happens."

"Oh, sure it does. What I meant was, she's just fantastically pretty. It must be so great, living with somebody like that, somebody who lets you go your own way. I mean, she gives you your own private *space*."

"Sure," Julie said. "Hey, did you memorize that list Miss Coleman handed out?"

51

Cindy rolled her eyes. "I took it to bed last night and fell asleep, beating my brains over it. Woke up with a kink in my neck, you wouldn't believe."

A few seconds after the bell, the teacher appeared, looking more harried than usual. She was still buttoning her lab smock as she hurried to her desk. For the first part of the period, she reviewed the experiment they had begun on Monday. Then she peered at them over her glasses. "Any questions? Okay, let's get back to our project."

Julie joined the others clustering around Miss Coleman as she directed a new girl on the correct procedure in dissecting a frog. Mary Lou, a tall freckled redhead, had recently come from Texas. Yesterday, Julie had grinned at her obvious distress. But she alone heard the girl's soft dismayed comment.

Now, Mary Lou's face looked grim, and she swallowed hard. Watching her, Julie thought, maybe she could get her off the hook. The boys were always charmed when one of the girls had to make a sudden dash for the bathroom.

Breaking the heavy silence, she replayed Mary Lou's anguished words of the day before. "Nevah saw anythin' moh revoltin' in mah entiah life — a li'l green livvah in a *frawwwg* — !"

The class exploded into laughter, Miss Coleman finally wiping her eyes on the hem of her smock. "Julie, you're heading for a great career," she said at last, "but I doubt it'll be in the field of science." She chuckled. "I locked up early last night to watch the tryouts. After the way you perform in class, I couldn't resist. And I must say, your sketches were really fine."

She paused. "That reminds me. For those of you who *are* attuned to this particular field, how many are interested in exhibits for the spring Science Fair? Let's have a show of hands."

The bell rang a few minutes later. No one but Julie seemed to notice that Mary Lou had taken advantage of the discussion to slip quietly from the room.

CHAPTER 6

After the last class, Julie talked to Nick for several minutes at her locker, exchanging the notes they were beginning to write to each other. He illustrated his with cartoon figures. Hers were usually in rhyme, silly limericks or fractured fairy tales in verse.

Today, he laughed as he glanced at the heading on the slip of paper she handed to him. CINDERELLA IS A LAID-BACK LADY.

Below, she had printed:

> So meek and sweet, she'd make you sick
> This prim unliberated chick
> But when she got her chance to fly
> (She didn't even know the guy
> Before they met and shared a dance)
> And still she up and took a chance.
> She said she'd wed, fulfill his wishes
> If *he* would always do the dishes
> She must have been a foxy broad,
> But Cinderella was a fraud!

"Yeah," he said, "I'll go along with that." He looked at her, smiling faintly, curiosity in his eyes. "How long did it take you to put this one together?"

Julie shrugged. "It seemed to fit what Miss Fitzgerald was *not* saying in Family Living. Hey, I got so involved, I didn't get the homework assignment. Did you?"

"Sure." He flipped open his notebook and held it out so she could copy the scrawled instructions at the bottom of the page. "You should worry about a class like that," he said. "What difference will it make ten years from now?"

She grinned, amused by the contrast between Nick's casual reaction when she goofed off, and the put-down she could inevitably expect from Tony. "Thanks," she said. "Gotta run. I hear Mr. Lawton starts those classes at four o'clock sharp."

The last bus departed as she rounded the corner and headed for the gym. She decided she had time to duck into the bathroom. While she was still in the cubicle at the end, she heard the outer door open and a familiar squeal of laughter.

Betty Jo exclaimed then in her sullen husky voice, "Somebody like that can get to be a real drag, though. Miss Coleman thinks she's so cute, she gets away with murder."

Julie froze. The two girls from biology class. Were they talking about her?

A moment later, Cindy confirmed her suspicions. "Well, I thought she was kind of funny today," she said in the conciliatory tone she adopted whenever someone took issue with her views. "But the thing at tryouts, that was really rotten. Gloria Bellfort said Miss Varilla's face got all red. The minute that tall guy started singing — you know, the country western thing we thought was so awful — well, she walked out." A trill of laughter. "I bet she gives old Julie fourteen laps around the track the next time she pulls something in P.E."

"I hope I'm there to see it." Betty Jo again. "You got a match?"

"Why should I carry matches? I don't smoke." Then, in a softer tone, Cindy added, "No, but I think I put some in my locker for you."

"That's a great big huge help. Oh, come on. The way the wind's blowing, your hair's just gonna get all messed up again."

The outer door closed. Moments later, Julie emerged to tear across the lawn to the gym. Mr. Lawton had just finished taking roll as she slid onto the end seat of the closest bleacher. He glanced at her and nodded, but said nothing.

She let out her breath slowly, feeling her face burn as a few heads turned to look at her, curious. Almost late for the very first class, she thought, anger a fiery lump in her chest. Those miserable *losers* had delayed her just long enough so Mr. Lawton had been aware of her last-minute entrance.

Why hadn't she come out of the booth? Why hadn't she come out and simply stood there, staring at them, letting them know she'd heard every word? She thought with inner loathing, because she was a card-carrying chicken, that's why. She curled up at the edges just picturing something like that. Clearly, she didn't have any more guts than she had taste.

Not now, she told herself. There would be time later to deal with her feelings about the unpleasant incident in the girls' room. It wasn't the first time she had become aware that people talked about her behind her back. It didn't even hurt as much, because she had never considered Cindy and Betty Jo close friends. More than once, she had discovered with considerable pain that girls she really liked ripped her the moment her back was turned. Then again, there were friends like Teresa who made the sorting-out process worthwhile.

With a vast effort, she forced her attention to the teacher.

"In case you're wondering about our guest — " He nodded in her direction. "She is sitting in to observe these sessions at my invitation. She will not participate in class activities.

"Now then — " He paused to prop one foot on a bleacher. "Let's talk about talent. Sometimes it can be a problem."

He leaned forward, studying them. "It's — a matter of learning bad habits. In many creative fields, music and literature and art, for instance, if you indulge your talent without learning your craft first, you may be heading for trouble.

"All the wrong bits of business, all the sloppy little routines you've acquired are going to have to be stripped away. When you're down to bare essentials, you begin all over again, building at that point with the solid fundamental tools of your trade, learning the proper technique."

His face softened with his brief, appealing smile. "In this class, at your ages, I don't think you've had time to acquire too many layers of poor training or bad habits. I want to take you as you are, as I find you, and help develop and shape your latent talent. Yes, I'm pretty sure you have an average amount of that, or you wouldn't be here after school wasting your time. And mine."

Julie thought about that in the short silence that ensued. *Bad habits*, she mused. He had mentioned discipline to her last night. Did he discuss that with everyone? Or had he seen the evidence of bad habits in the sketches she had presented?

"We'll do vocal exercises," Mr. Lawton continued, "to teach you to ar-ti-cu-late." He repeated the word in a higher, then a lower register. "We'll do improvisations, a group situation. You'll have fun, I promise you, but the basic function of improvs at the beginning is to show me what you can do. And what you can learn to do better. I want you to relax and be yourselves. You aren't going to be acting right away, getting inside another person. Time enough for that when you find out who you are."

Completely involved now, Julie felt the words spark excitement that flashed through her like a shiver. Yes, she thought, he could teach her what she wanted to know. She would learn the secret here.

She watched, fascinated, as the class did pantomimes, what the teacher called "exercises in body language." He had them doing the arm movements in swimming, telling them they were a mile from shore and must conserve their energy. A moment later, he snapped at them that time had become important now. They had almost reached shallow water, and there was a vital message to deliver.

Arms swung faster past tense, reddening faces. At the signal to stop, a murmur of soft, self-conscious laughter swept through the group. Then, after a brief rest period, each member of the class stood on tiptoe, stretching, fingers extended.

"You're reaching for apples," Mr. Lawton said. "Just a little more, and you'll grab the big juicy one at the end of the branch."

Another ripple of laughter.

Julie propped an elbow on one knee as she watched, chin in her palm. He gave them a specific direction, she thought. And then he gave them something definite to do with it. It became more than a stretching exercise when they pretended to reach for apples.

She studied the teacher with awed respect, and again she felt an inner thrill of anticipation. It had been fantastic luck, Mr. Lawton coming here to Mesa Verde, inviting her to sit in on his class, even before she was eligible to take it.

Exercise period over, the teacher explained the

first group improvisation. They were to be people in an airport waiting room, he told the class. They could decide for themselves what they were doing there, how they would behave.

Then he turned and came toward Julie. Her breath jolted at the back of her throat, and she felt her smile tremble as he sat down beside her.

"Go ahead," he said to the students milling around on the floor of the gym. "You'll need a minute to get yourselves sorted out."

He gave Julie a crooked smile. "Enright. What have you picked up so far?"

She took a deep steadying breath. "Well — well, the exercises would be good in a lot of ways, I guess. Physically, I mean, keeping limber. And — and pantomime — that's always good, I suppose — " She couldn't seem to think of another word but "good." She sounded retarded, she thought, then flushed as she recalled that the teacher, himself, had a retarded child.

"Mmm," he said, studying the class, eyes narrowed. "Anything else?"

Without stopping to examine her ideas further, she blurted, "It seemed to me as if — well, I noticed that you seem to give them an exercise to do and then — then you give them a reason for doing it. So it turns into something more than — " She broke off as he turned to stare at her.

"Did you read that somewhere?" he asked bluntly. "Did somebody tell you — ?" He saw her shake her head, bewildered. "Then I have to say, Enright, that's a rather remarkable observation." He grinned at her as he got to his feet. "Don't look so scared. I meant, it was a remarkably good observation."

Julie sat, wrapped in the warm glow of his approval. As he returned to the class, her mind closed around the words, memorizing the inflection of that magnificent voice, the smile in his eyes.

Then she put the moment aside for future appraisal. She wasn't sure what she had said that was all that extraordinary, but she would figure it out later. Now, she listened intently as he commented on the unfolding improv — that's what he had called it — as each student acted out a certain form of behavior.

"Peterson and Smith, the lovebirds about to be parted. Yes, good. Peterson looking brave, chin up, waiting to cry later. It's okay, dear, he'll be back tomorrow." Giggles, a soft whistle from the sidelines.

"Smith, you're putting your heart and soul into that last embrace, but you're enjoying it a bit too much. Look, man, you won't be seeing her for a whole day. That's it — suffer a little." Ginny Peterson put her hand over her mouth, shoulders shaking, as Howie Smith tried to look agonized but stoical.

Mr. Lawton paced among them, slowly. "Atkins, the executive type late for an appointment. Ulcer acting up. Why can't they run this crummy airline like he runs his business? Popping anti-acid mints — I trust that's what they are — good, Atkins."

In the space of a few minutes, he had analyzed each pantomime, casual humor in his remarks. But to Julie, his suggestions seemed incisive, of immense value. She noticed that he touched very lightly on the performances of the two shy members of the class. Leaning close to Jerry Hawkins, he said something that made Jerry grin and turn as red as his T-shirt. Linda Gaylord blushed, too, when he put his hand on her shoulder. "Fine. That was just fine," he said, and the girl's wondering gaze followed him.

It was over then, with the distribution of copies of the first play, *You're a Good Man, Charlie Brown*. A few students clustered around Mr. Lawton to ask questions. The rest straggled toward the door.

Dorie Kaiser, a short, stocky blonde in a tight beige dress, paused in front of Julie for a moment, staring at her. "So you got an invite to hang around — how'd you manage that?"

Julie bit back a sharp reply. Dorie had a mean tongue. Most of the kids joked about her colorful vocabulary, but few of them cared to tangle with her.

"Ah — I guess Mr. Lawton thought I was, you know, interested."

"I bet he did." There was a sneer in Dorie's harsh voice. "Little Sara Heartburn, can't wait to get to Hollywood. The old casting-couch routine. You oughta do just great."

Julie felt her cheeks blazing in instant reflection of the anger surging inside. She got to her feet and hurried toward the door, the sound of Dorie's scornful laughter drifting after her.

It still echoed in her memory as she turned onto her block, a counterpoint to a rerun of the conversation inadvertently overheard in the girls' room. " — *gets away with murder — the next time she pulls something in P.E. — hope I'm there to see it —* "

"Julie? Julie!"

She turned to see Teresa running down the street after her. She had promised to stop and fill Teresa in about the drama class. But even before she left the schoolground, Julie had decided she'd better wait until later. In her present mood, she wouldn't be fit company for anybody but a lynching party — that is, if she could nominate the lynchee.

Teresa slowed as she came closer, dark eyes searching her friend's face. "What happened? Julie, what's wrong?"

"Nothing that bad." She tried to smile and knew from Teresa's expression that she hadn't been too successful. "Just a couple of things all in one day. I mean, I could have handled them if they'd been — spaced out a little."

She sighed. "Got trapped in the john while Cindy and Betty Jo did a number on me. And then — just now, Dorie Kaiser got on my back. While I was still bleeding from — oh, let's not talk about it. Please. I'll just bawl."

"Maybe that's what you should do," Teresa said softly, her hand on Julie's arm. "I keep telling you, it isn't any good to hold that stuff inside. Julie, it'll just chew you up."

"No, it won't." This time, the smile came easier. "People like that? Why waste a lot of emotion on those turkeys?"

"Listen," Teresa said after a moment. "Your aunt called, said she had to go to L.A. and she won't be back till tomorrow. So Mom said you should pack your bag and come spend the night. We can talk. It's really good timing." She added firmly, "Later on, we can talk."

Julie stood for a moment, undecided. "Okay," she said at last. "Great. Want to come with me while I get my stuff?"

A half hour later, she followed Teresa through the front door of the big house on the corner, tossed her case on the couch, and ran to the kitchen to hug Mama Angel.

"You are a neat lady to adopt me again," she said. "Something smells super fantastic. I promise I'll eat as much as Tony. I will *scarf* down the groceries. Because you are not only beautiful, but the best cook in the entire state of California!"

Mama Martone beamed. "She will eat," she crooned. "Farfalla will eat tonight."

In the middle of the big warm kitchen, full of a heavenly spicy fragrance, Julie saw Teresa's mother smiling at her with obvious affection. And for a moment, her world swung back again into the sunshine.

CHAPTER 7

A sudden sharp scratching sound woke her.
Julie lay rigid for a moment, orienting herself.
Yes, this was Teresa's bedroom. Her friend's
hair was a dark shadow on the pillow in the
other bed. A branch of the persimmon tree outside had brushed against the window.

On the chest of drawers across the room, the
luminous hands of a small clock said it was
nearly midnight. She must have slept hard, Julie
thought, because her mind was wide awake now,
alert. She might have difficulty dozing off again.

Teresa made a gentle buzzing noise, then
sighed softly and turned over. Julie smiled, hoping her dreams were happy ones. Such a super
person, Teresa, always seeing the best in people
and making allowances for the ones who were a
long way from perfect.

The branch touched the window again, and

Julie shivered, wishing she'd brought her flannel pajamas. But the seam in one sleeve had ripped in the wash on Saturday, and she hadn't had time to mend it. Now, acutely aware that her feet were freezing, she knew she would have to get up. Whenever her feet got cold, she had to go to the bathroom.

A few minutes later, she padded back down the hall. On impulse, before she climbed in bed, she pulled the drape from the window to look outside.

Fog! A quick breath caught in her throat. She could barely see the outline of the persimmon tree. Gray ribbons of mist hovered around the top branches, but when she looked toward the ground, all she could see was a churning layer of white. She pulled the drape closed after one horrified glance, her heart pounding painfully.

Without making a conscious decision, knowing only that she wouldn't sleep, that she couldn't stay in the small closed-in bedroom another minute, she went out to grope her way to the living room.

She stood for a moment, shivering convulsively. Then she remembered the big afghan Mrs. Martone had just finished. Yes, it was there, draped across the back of the couch. Huddled within the soft folds, she tucked her icy feet beneath her. In the fireplace across the room, dying embers winked through the darkness.

Julie buried her nose in the woolly material, imagining she could smell Mama Angel's fragrance, one part the light carnation perfume she favored, the rest a unique distillation of herself, a warm, loving woman.

Footsteps pattered down the hall. Her eyes adjusted now to the dim light from the glowing remnants of the fire, Julie saw the outline of a short rounded figure in the door.

"Julie? Is that you?"

"Oh, Mama Angel, did I wake you?" she said softly. "I tried to be quiet."

Mrs. Martone closed the hall door and came noiselessly across the shag carpet. "I haven't been asleep. Tony isn't in yet. What's the matter, child? Aren't you feeling well?" She put a plump hand on Julie's forehead. "Like ice, you are. Weren't there enough blankets on your bed?"

"Oh, yes, I was okay. But I woke up and — " She hesitated. "I looked out the window and — "

Mama Angel made a slight sound. "The fog," she said. "Of course." She knew about the recurring dream. Once, several years ago, Julie had spent the night and wakened from the nightmare, sobbing. A distressed Teresa had gone to get her mother.

It had been so wonderful, Julie thought, recalling that night, to be cuddled and comforted as if she were a small child, not a big girl almost twelve.

Mrs. Martone crossed to the fireplace and began building up a new fire. "No trouble at all," she said when Julie protested. "I'm a night owl, anyway. My legs bother me sometimes, and nothing seems to help but pacing the floor. We'll just sit by the fire and have a cup of chocolate. When you're all warm again, inside and out, I think you'll be able to get back to sleep." She smiled as Julie came to curl on the braided hearth rug. "You stay right there while I fix our snack."

By the time she returned with steaming mugs and a dish of sesame seed cookies on a tray, flames were licking around the smaller chunks of wood and giving off a welcome warmth. Firelight flickered across her round pleasant face, and she sighed contentedly as she sank into the chair Julie brought for her.

"Now, isn't this cozy? For once, I have someone to keep me company. They sleep like logs, this family, every last one of them."

If she hadn't been disturbed, Mama Angel might be sleeping just as soundly, Julie suspected. She liked to think her own mother would have been like Teresa's, surrounding her with affection and concern if something troubled her or when she was ill.

In memory, her aunt's bright voice intruded, briefly diminishing her pleasure in this moment. "Can't abide whiney sick kids," Roz had said once. "Hot sticky hands and runny noses and big accusing eyes. Luckily, you were over all the spots and itches and whooping-on-the-rug stuff by the time you came to live here. You've been a most satisfactory child. Healthy as a horse, just like me."

Julie sipped her hot chocolate warily. Then she felt a gentle hand on her shoulder.

"Do you still have that dream?"

She nodded.

"Often?"

Julie lifted her head to look into the dark searching eyes. "Oh — maybe once a month."

"Often." It was a whisper, almost inaudible. Her hand touched Julie's cheek. "Have you ever thought there might be a reason it keeps coming back?"

For a second, Julie stiffened. But this was not her aunt, and Mama Angel laughed comfortably about something like psychology, insisting it was only a fancy name for common sense and human nature. In Julie's opinion, she was a lady who knew a lot more than people who wrote off-the-wall books analyzing everything to death.

"The accident was awful," she said, her voice quiet. "Really heavy for a little kid. But lots of people go through stuff like that. You can't cry the rest of your life."

A short silence.

"It helps to cry," Mrs. Martone said. "We've talked about this before. Expressing grief — that means to press out, to get your feelings out so they won't eat at you inside."

"I did cry," Julie said flatly. "I was only ten. Why should I cry now for something that happened six years ago? That sure wouldn't make me stop dreaming."

"No, perhaps not. Because you've accepted the fact that your parents are gone. Julie, you're a bright girl. You're a lot more sensible than — " she hesitated " — than a lot of girls your age."

"No, I'm still not sure where I'm at. But it wasn't easy for my aunt, you know, taking me in, disrupting her life."

In the echo of the words, she realized that she had replied, a bit defensively, to what she suspected Mama Angel had started to say: "You're a lot more sensible than your aunt."

The burning wood snapped loudly, an explosion of sparks flying up the chimney. "Roz always says any kid raised perfectly — terrific parents, everything squared away — well, that could be a bad trip too. How would that prepare them for a world where nothing's anywhere near perfect?"

Mrs. Martone made a soft neutral sound. "There is that," she said. "I just can't help but wonder about that dream — about those tears inside you — all those unshed tears. You are sobbing in the dream, searching for — what does a person search for, Julie? For something they've lost. But how many people keep on looking when they have accepted the fact that something is gone forever?"

Julie stared at her. *Something lost*, she thought. Spooky, how Mama Angel had picked up on that. "Do you mean — are you saying I lost something else that night? I mean, aside from my mother and father?"

"Well, didn't you? To my mind, you lost a way of life, as well. You remember your parents. Would they have raised you — as you are being raised now?"

Julie sighed. "No. For sure." She looked into the fire, sipped her hot drink. "I just wish — well, I don't want to take any cheap shots at you and Big Tony — you know I wouldn't do that. But if that's what I'm still looking for, a whole other way of life, I'd like something in between no rules at all and — and too many restrictions that don't make a lot of sense." She glanced at the woman watching her, at the faint smile on the round face. "Wouldn't that be better? Something in between?"

"Perhaps." The soft voice sounded tactful, tolerant, but unconvinced. "At least you know one thing, Farfalla. There are so many people who truly care about you — " She broke off as Julie sat up straight, the sudden movement nearly spilling her chocolate.

"This family, sure," she said evenly. "You're all great. I always know I can count on you. Even Tony, all the time trying to shape me up. But he's actually a very steady solid sort of person." She thought Mrs. Martone had made a low sound of amusement, but when she glanced at her, the dark eyes were quite serious.

"The thing is, I totally mess up sometimes. If I don't stop to think — and I never do. When you hurt people — well, that's so rotten." She saw Mama Angel shaking her head in obvious disbelief. "*I do*," Julie said in a small fierce voice. She blurted out the story of her impromptu impression of the P.E. teacher during the talent tryouts.

71

"A hard thing to learn, to bridle one's tongue," Mama Angel said. She sighed. "We say something in anger or sorrow, even from blind love because we want the best for people we love. But how can anyone be sure what's right for someone else?"

Julie knew she was speaking now about Tony and his father. Holding her breath, she gazed into the fire rather than at the source of the voice that held so much pain.

"All I can tell you, Julie, is that everyone gets hurt once in a while and most of us are guilty of hurting in turn. We would cut out our tongues before we would hurt a loved one, and yet — grown people are just as likely to say something and live to wish they could take it back. Those girls you overheard, maybe they're jealous of you."

After a moment, she chuckled. "I think you're being too hard on yourself. I've seen you do other things on the spur of the moment when you only wanted to cheer somebody up, make them laugh. Don't you think some of that helps to cancel out the business with Miss Varilla?"

In Julie's mind, she saw the grim face of the new girl from Texas. Getting Mary Lou off the hook today in biology earned one Brownie point, maybe, but hardly enough to make up for the incident at tryouts. Still, she began to feel a little better.

In a high Julie Andrews voice, she recited primly:

"Yes, my name is Mary Poppins
I'm a busy little bee
There's no one in this whole wide world
As adorable as me."

"You should better believe it," said Mrs. Martone firmly.

Julie grinned. Sometimes it irritated her when adults tried to imitate the way kids talked, but Mama Angel just tickled her. The odd thing was how much it bothered her when Roz did it. Her aunt was word perfect when it came to the casual language of kids. On her worst day, Roz would never say anything like, *You should better believe it*.

A few minutes later, she heard a car in the drive, then a few fervent words in Italian from Mrs. Martone. With a prickle of guilt, Julie realized for the first time that Mama Angel had been listening anxiously for that sound. Tony had been out there in thick fog, driving through it. Immersed in her own trivial woes, she had given him only a fleeting thought.

She turned to smile at his mother. "You've been worried," she said, her voice soft with regret. "Here I've been bending your ear about my dumb problems and — "

"No, no, no." Mrs. Martone laughed. "Never any trouble, worrying about one more. You did me a favor, Farfalla, taking my mind off the fog and Tony out in it. Thank God, here he is home safe."

The front door opened, and the flames flickered in the wave of cold moist air that swept toward them. Tony stood, hands on hips, surveying the scene.

"Looks like a better party than the one across town. I should have stayed home. What's the big — ?" He glanced at Julie. "Oh. The fog. Just rolled in an hour ago." He came to pop a cooky in his mouth and said around it, "Got any more chocolate, Ma?"

"Of course." His mother got to her feet and touched his arm lightly. "Sit down and warm yourself there on the rug."

He shed his coat and sat down beside Julie, jackknifed so he could put his chin on his knees.

"Tony Martone," she muttered. "Not only a C.B. but the biggest MCP from here to the border."

"C.B. — Citizens Band — which I don't have. It means something else?"

"Better you shouldn't ask." She scowled at him. "Worrying your poor mother, coming in this late. There she is out in the kitchen waiting on you. And with your luck, you'll marry somebody wacko enough to iron your underwear and scratch your back three times a day."

He changed positions to present her with a back that looked a yard wide in the Pendleton shirt that had once been Big Tony's. "Start between my shoulder blades," he said, "and work down gradually."

Instead, she grabbed his sides, knowing how ticklish he was. She and Teresa could reduce him to groaning pleas for mercy when they ganged up on him.

Without Teresa, however, she found herself outmatched. In a matter of seconds, Tony had his arms around her, both her hands imprisoned behind her back. Then he leaned over to blow gently down her neck just beneath her ear in the place where he knew *she* was most ticklish.

"Tony!" she squeaked. "That isn't fair! I didn't even get a good grip on you — Tony!"

He moved his head to kiss her lightly, drew back to look at her, then kissed her again. No gentle teasing kiss this time, but something neither of them expected. Certainly, Julie had never suspected she would respond with lightning intensity when a wrestling match with Tony turned into something else again. Not Tony!

They drew apart seconds before Mrs. Martone came back with the rattling tray.

"Here we are. More cookies. And cheese and crackers. And fruit if you're really hungry."

Julie got to her feet, her face burning, hoping Mama Angel would blame that on the heat from the fire. "mmMMM!" she said quickly. "Fat City. Mama Angel, I'll pass. I think I can sleep now." She leaned to kiss the soft round cheek. "Thanks for listening," she murmured. "It really helped."

Then she ran down the hall. She wanted to be alone, to get into bed and try to figure out what had happened, how that kiss had got out of control.

CHAPTER 8

Teresa shook her awake the next morning, laughing as Julie tried to bury her head under the pillow. "Come on, sleepyhead. You've got fifteen minutes to get dressed. Mom said to let you sleep till the last minute, and that's right now. Julie, you hear me? I said you've got fifteen—"

"I hear you, I hear you. Fifteen—" Julie blinked and sat up. "Wow! Is the shower clear?"

Teresa grinned at her. "Traffic's been light for the last half hour. You've got toast and hot chocolate coming in three minutes. Curb service right here while you dress. Now get it in gear and *go*."

Julie flew. A fast shower, skipping a shampoo — no time for that — and she skidded back to the bedroom to throw on her clothes. Munching toast as she zipped jeans and buttoned her

T-shirt, she thought, bless Mama Angel for letting her sleep late. She sure hadn't looked forward to facing Tony across the breakfast table. It would be bad enough driving to school with him.

The hairbrush in midair, she paused to peer at her flushed face in the mirror over the chest of drawers. *Shape up*, she whispered fiercely to her reflection. She mustn't give Tony the idea that kiss had been any big deal.

Last night before she dropped off to sleep, she had decided it was merely a matter of biology. A girl and a boy wrestling on the rug like a couple of little kids and — Mother Nature took over. Simple as that.

She nodded firmly, then finished the chocolate in the big yellow mug, a ceramic mug with a picture of a butterfly on it. Mama Angel had brought it home from an arts and crafts show, producing it with a flourish the next time Julie stayed for lunch.

At least one good thing had happened yesterday, Julie thought, and leaned toward the mirror to apply lip gloss. Her talk with Teresa's mother had been enormously comforting. As for Tony kissing her, well, no big thing. She'd set him straight in a hurry if he tried to make anything of it.

In the car a few minutes later, she felt a perverse irritation, however, because Tony acted as if nothing at all had happened. In fact, he was his usual obnoxious self, doing a horrible imitation of John Wayne all the way to school.

"I tell you, litt-ul sweethearts, it's gonna be a horse race. Who's gonna be the Homecoming Queen? That's the question."

"I know," Julie said brightly. "You're doing Howard Cosell, right?"

"That's cool." He glared over his shoulder at his giggling twin. "Professional jealousy, huh, Jule? All pushed out of shape the minute somebody comes along with real talent."

"No, no, I've got it now. Don Rickles!" She saw his grin in the rearview mirror. "You have to admit, Tony, nobody expects this kind of thing from you. Not when you're always demonstrating an obvious talent for — "

Luckily, an old VW provided a distraction at that moment, darting in front of the Toyota just as Tony started to turn in to the school. He leaned out the window and bellowed angrily at the other driver, a tiny girl who could barely see over the wheel. She paid no attention to him or to the other cars that honked at her as she drove erratically across the parking lot.

Julie heard Teresa gasp. She hadn't reacted, herself, to anything but the echo of her last words. *An obvious talent for* — how long would it be before they could both forget the silly incident in front of the fire last night? As she told Tony's mother, she had no talent at all for pausing to think before she spoke. Now, she thought, annoyed, for a while everything would seem to have a double meaning. Wasn't her life complicated enough without that?

Nick was waiting by her locker, and she

greeted him with special warmth kindled by guilt. "Nicko! There was someone on the Channel 10 movie last night who looked so much like you, it was unreal."

"Redford? Donnie Osmond?" He pretended to rack his brain. "Sure," he said, "Woody Allen."

"Nah. Your eyes are a different color."

Nick shrugged. "Reminds me, have you seen his latest? I thought maybe Friday night — "

"Yes!" She smiled at him. "I think maybe Friday night will be great."

He reached past her to close her locker, and they headed toward Advisory. "Hey," he said, "nominations for Homecoming Queen coming up next week. Are you ready to reign?"

Her aunt, the Martone twins, and Nick all seemed to assume she was a shoo-in for princess, but Julie didn't feel that sure about it. There were too many Betty Jos and Cindys around, she thought, people who only pretended to be her friends.

The election of a Homecoming Queen, always a senior, and the princesses from each grade was supposed to be based on the candidates' school spirit. Actually, it was pretty much a beauty and popularity contest. Julie thought uneasily, she couldn't be considered a hot contender in either category. Now if they had a special division for someone with hoof-in-mouth disease, no sweat.

By the time third period rolled around, she had begun to feel the effects of her sketchy night's sleep. Her eyes burned, and she had to struggle to stay awake in geometry while the teacher droned on and on explaining some obscure equation.

She entered the biology lab, too weary to work up even a minor irritation when Cindy and Betty Jo called to her amiably.

"Hey, Julie, Mary Lou's looking for you."

"Know what Miss Coleman calls you? The class cut-up."

"You're next in line to practice on the frog." Betty Jo gave her a sly smile.

Julie groaned and put her head down on her arms to discourage further conversation. A moment later, she felt a hand on her shoulder, and she jerked up, ready to let fly this time. But it was neither Cindy or Betty Jo who stood peering down at her.

The tall freckled girl from Texas said with genuine concern, "Honey, aren't you feelin' well?"

Julie brushed her hair back from her forehead. "Just tired," she said. "I didn't get much sleep last night."

"Oh. Well, you better catch up tonight." Her voice flowed as slowly as honey from a jar. "I'm Mary Lou Montgomery. I just wanted to thank you for, you know, makin' a *diversion* yesterday. Honey, I was turnin' as green as that li'l *critter* about that time. And I figured you *detected* that. It was just the *kindest* thing for you to do — "

Julie laughed. "I can't really get off on the autopsy bit, myself," she said. "Grosses me out.

You can return the favor when they hand me the scalpel, okay?"

Mary Lou's green eyes widened. "Sure thing," she said. "What'll I do? Get the hiccups or faint?"

"Whatever seems right." Julie looked at her and realized abruptly that the slender redhead was serious. "I'm kidding," she said. "It isn't anything I can't handle. But thanks. You really meant it, didn't you?"

A nod followed by a long sigh. "There'd be only one thing worse than losin' my breakfast," Mary Lou said solemnly, "and that'd be losin' it right *here*. I mean, in front of everybody. I jus' wanted you to know I thought it was a real nice thing, you *rescuin'* me like that."

She went up the aisle to stop and talk to Betty Jo and Cindy before she settled herself on her stool in front. Julie watched her for a moment with a faint smile. When she stopped to think about it, Mary Lou seemed to be surprisingly popular considering her brief time at Mesa Verde. More and more often in the corridors, Julie noticed her laughing and chattering with a group of kids. She could understand that now, knowing Mary Lou better. A terrific girl, she thought, warm and unaffected, the kind it would be nice to have as a friend.

After class, Miss Coleman glanced at her and beckoned. "Julie? May I see you a minute?"

As Julie approached, the teacher searched for a pencil, found it behind her ear, then sat looking at it as if she'd forgotten why she wanted it.

"There's a test next week," she said at last. "You need a good grade on it. I hope you'll buckle down and study. Read the chapters and learn the vocabulary list."

Julie winced. "I will. I'll be up for it, I promise."

Miss Coleman smiled. "I think it's only fair to tell you, Mr. Lawton's been around to check on you. He's very conscientious about his students, and perhaps even more so about — well, you aren't officially a member of his class, I understand. You're — auditing the drama program?"

Julie nodded.

"Fine. Good experience with your obvious bent for the performing arts. But I'm sure he's told you that you'll have to keep up your work in other classes or — "

As she paused, Julie said stiffly, "Yes. Yes, he told me."

The teacher looked at her for a moment over the absurd Ben Franklin glasses. "I know how much it must mean to you," she said. Her voice was so quiet, it was almost lost in the clamor from the corridor. "That's why I'm hoping you get — a very good grade on the test next week."

"Yes," Julie said again. "Thanks, Miss Coleman."

But as she hurried for her next class, she felt more annoyance than gratitude. Everybody pushing and shoving, she thought. Get in line for a shot at Enright. Mr. Lawton sure hadn't wasted any time setting her up, either.

She told Teresa and Nick about it at lunch. "Is that heavy?" she concluded on a note of disgust. "He spelled it out Monday night, didn't he? Now why do I get the distinct impression that he's leaning on me?"

Teresa made a face. "I doubt that he means it like that, Julie. It's only that he's professional. I mean, with his background in the theater — really dedicated and disciplined."

"Tell me about it," Julie said glumly.

Nick stacked the empty milk cartons on his tray. "Give him a few more months," he advised. "A little more mileage, and he'll relax. New teachers and brand new boots, you gotta break 'em in, that's all. He's just gung ho to make a point, way I figure."

"He's made it. Twice. I can't believe him, making the rounds of all my teachers and — " She reached for a milk carton and squashed it with unnecessary violence. "Ultimatums," she muttered. "Talk about a power trip — "

In her mind, she heard her aunt's amused voice. "Show me a man who issues ultimatums, and I'll show you a man who's married to his job. Because you better believe he's somebody's ex-husband. Who needs that kind of power trip?"

Well, maybe Roz was right, Julie thought, but she pushed the brief moment of recall to the back of her mind. It bothered her lately each time she discovered an element of truth in her aunt's blithe but cynical observation. A frustrating process when someone consistently knocked the props from beneath something you were trying to build.

Julie examined the idea briefly. Building? What was she building? My life, she thought. And then with a sudden surge of anger, why couldn't people let her find her own answers? Did they have to be the same for everybody? Hadn't Roz made mistakes, royally messing up her own life?

In the wake of the rebellious anger came the inevitable tide of guilt. Nothing like missing a little sleep, she thought, then dragging around all day snapping at everybody like a nasty-tempered pup. Bad enough to do it out loud, but somehow it left an aching sore place inside when she raged in silence. Especially about a great person like Aunt Roz. With a distorted sense of loyalty like hers, the next thing she'd be taking aim at Mama Angel and Teresa. With relief, she heard the bell and got up to follow Nick as he headed down the aisle between the tables.

She stopped to grab Teresa's arm. "I'm sorry," she said. "I'm in a mean rotten mood. You should have made me eat by myself."

Her friend nodded. "Right. Out by the garbage cans." The great dark eyes were warm, amused. "Even in a bad mood, you're more fun than anybody else I know."

They separated at the door, and Julie had a swift glimpse of herself in the glass as it swung back against the dark green wall beyond. Laughing, her short fair hair blowing around her face, a girl who was — almost — pretty, she thought, startled.

Her rising spirits spiraled down once more with a chance encounter outside the library.

The door burst open and Mary Lou emerged, smiling as she saw Julie. "Hi!" she said. "This wind! It's about to freeze my *bones*."

Greg Horton followed her out, his smile disappearing as he glanced at Julie. "Come on," he said impatiently and put his hand on Mary Lou's arm to propel her past.

Julie walked toward her English class, trying to sort out her feelings. Yes, she was disappointed, she thought. No chance now that she and Mary Lou could be friends. Greg would see to that.

What did the girl from Texas see in him, anyway? To be fair about it, the same things she had, probably. He had money and that neat car, and he wasn't bad looking. And he was so bright, he had fascinated her at first. She found herself hoping that someone would warn Mary Lou about his drinking, however. She was new at Mesa Verde, and it could be rough for a while in a different school. You had no way of knowing things like that until you got to know people who could set you straight. Well, she wouldn't have to worry about Mary Lou in that case, because it was clear she had already made dozens of friends.

Still, the incident stirred up all the unpleasant prickling little feelings inside just after Teresa had calmed them down. A few minutes later, the English teacher called on her to continue the reading of *Julius Caesar* which the class had begun yesterday.

"I would have had thee there, and here again, ere I can tell thee what thou shouldst do there. O constancy, be strong upon my side," Julie read obediently.

The words were Portia's, but rendered in a skillful long-practiced impression of the soft breathless voice of Marilyn Monroe.

CHAPTER 9

She had intended to study hard for the biology test, promising herself as well as Miss Coleman that she would know the material by next week. Yet somehow, the time got away from her.

For one thing, the afterschool drama sessions were really interesting now that people were reading for the play. Julie listened, intrigued, to an exchange between Mr. Lawton and the stocky blonde boy who had been chosen for the lead.

"I just don't feel comfortable about it, Mr. Lawton. Maybe I still don't have it straight. You say to be myself, but how can I be me and play Charlie Brown? I'm Steve Culver, not — "

The teacher held up his hand, smiling. "It's easier than you think, because you're playing a character in Mr. Schulz's head, not a real person. It would be more difficult if you were Julius

Caesar or — let's come down to someone more contemporary — Buffalo Bill, for instance. Everybody has an image of old Bill in his big hat, the long white hair, the elegant suit. There he was in his later years, on horseback, charging around some arena. All the actors who play Buffalo Bill have to make themselves fit that image, right?"

Steve nodded, but he still looked puzzled.

"Okay," Mr. Lawton said. His hand flipped as he went on with his explanation. "Now, Hamlet could be ninety years old or black. Juliet might be a two-hundred-pound lady. Neither of them were real people, you see, except in Mr. Shakespeare's imagination. What the actor plays is Hamlet's *philosophy* — "

Listening, Julie took a deep breath. She found herself nodding as she realized what the teacher meant. For her impressions, she used the materials within her own character if they fit the person she tried to imitate. She molded the rest, body and voice and gestures, her hair and facial expressions, in as close a copy as she could manage.

But if she were to play Juliet or Lucy in the present play, she would have to work with far more subtle detail. Her only guidelines would be the character's personality and philosophy as someone had described them in words and comic strip drawings.

She found the concept strangely exciting. If you built a character from those materials, using yourself as a base, all those things unique to you alone, the end result would be something no one else could do, no one in the whole world.

With an effort, she brought herself back from the pursuit of an idea new and challenging to her.

"Steve," Mr. Lawton was saying, "suppose I asked you to play a gangster. Would you be Brando's Godfather — or one of Bogart's bad guys?"

Julie leaned forward, holding her breath now, afraid she would miss a word, a gesture, a faint inflection of that magical voice. In the space of a few seconds, with infinite skill, the teacher had given the two impressions as he spoke.

One moment, using his shoulders, the expression around his mouth and the slurred sound of the words that emerged, he transformed himself into Brando's Godfather. The next, through posture and the familiar harsh voice with the hint of a lisp, he was Bogart playing one of a long list of heavies.

"In that case," Mr. Lawton told Steve, "you'd be playing Brando or Bogart, not the gangster in the play. He wouldn't be *your* gangster. Not unless you made him yours with whatever bits of business you decided to bring to the character. That's all I mean when I say, be yourself, even though you're playing Charlie Brown. Clear?"

The boy nodded, smiling now in appreciation.

Somehow, the stimulation of those classes stayed with Julie. She found it almost impossible to concentrate on the dull chapters in the biology text, let alone memorize the long vocabulary list. She felt a vague alarm once she realized how far behind she had fallen. Two nights in a row, she made a serious attempt to read the material, but half an hour of it was all she could take.

She'd really get on it over the weekend, she told herself. After all, she was a quick study when it came to something like a script. Already she had memorized most of the play the drama class was still analyzing.

Biology had never been her favorite thing. When the lines in the textbook began to blur from overwhelming boredom, Julie leaned her head back against her pillows and let her mind drift in a brief refreshing respite.

Mr. Lawton's lectures would come back to her without so much as a syllable missing. She would think about an acting formula: listen, react, respond, recalling the teacher's instructions to the class, the demonstrations she found so impressive. And she would look at the clock and find the better part of two hours had gone by. No big thing, she told herself. Even if she took Friday night off for the movie with Nick, there was always the weekend.

She woke on Saturday with a headache and sore throat.

"You look like death warmed over," Roz said cheerfully when Julie staggered out for breakfast. "Stay away from me, sweetie. In fact, you better get right back to bed. I'll bring you a pitcher of juice and a thermos of tea. See if you can drown whatever bug you've got."

Julie croaked, "Just my luck. I've got so much to *do*."

"Oh, forget the house and laundry. I'll get to it tomorrow. Poor lamb, you look just awful."

"Thanks a lot. That really helps." Julie headed for the hall. "Homework, a test coming up next week, all that garbage," she muttered.

"That is the word," her aunt agreed briskly. "You pop back in bed and sleep it off, and we'll keep our fingers crossed you aren't too contagious. As far as homework goes, well, with your brains, Babe, not to worry. It may take you an hour and a half to catch up."

At the door, Julie turned to stare at her. Her aunt was wearing a new T-shirt. In front, it said *Yes!* in big red letters and *No!* in big blue letters. When Roz crossed to the sink, Julie read the big green letters on the back of the shirt, *Confused?* She sighed and headed for her room.

Actually, for the next three days, she felt too miserable to worry much about anything. Drifting in and out of a heavy fevered sleep, she got up only to go to the bathroom and drink quarts of juice and broth.

Eventually, on Monday, she got up and wandered through the house, feeling a little stronger but too restless to settle in one room for long. The place seemed cold and empty.

Roz had left a note saying she would be late, but she had left jello in the refrigerator and a thick pureed soup on the stove. It looked revolting, a kind of greenish brown, but to Julie it tasted terrific. By evening, she had consumed three bowls of it. She sat in the kitchen, debating the wisdom of washing her hair, when the phone rang.

"Thank goodness," Teresa said. "We've been really worried. First your aunt came by to say you were sick, then Nick said she really chewed him out for calling while you were asleep and — how *are* you?"

"Much better. I think I'll live. I'm just trying to decide if it's worth it."

"Silly. You sound good." Teresa sighed. "Angel wants to bring you a care package. She *knows* you aren't eating right. She *knows* if she'd been taking care of you, you'd be well by now."

Julie grinned. "If she'd been taking care of me," she said, "I probably wouldn't have been sick in the first place."

A gurgle of laughter came over the wire. "Right. You don't dare get sick around here. Angel looks you in the eye first thing in the morning and last thing at night. And then she points at you and says, *don't get sick!*" A soft giggle. "She's not here right now. Dad took her shopping."

"I figured." Julie smiled. The twins often called their mother Angel to tease her, but only when their father wasn't around.

"She told me to call you," Teresa said. "My instructions are to tell you *sternly*, don't you dare wash your hair."

"She reads my mind even when I'm not around."

"So do I. I sort of thought you'd be feeling better by now. And that's what you'd be thinking about. So don't. You aren't going to school tomorrow?"

Julie sighed. "I don't suppose I should. I'm still pretty wobbly. Did I miss much today?"

A short silence. "Test in biology."

"Damn. Miss Coleman'll be sure I stayed home on purpose."

"As long as your conscience is clear — "

"Well, it isn't. I wasn't anywhere near ready for that test. And the way I feel, I won't be ready for the makeup, either."

"I'll come down after school tomorrow," Teresa said. "I can help you with the vocabulary list. Okay?"

"Sure, thanks."

"Julie?"

"Yeah?"

"Don't wash your hair tonight."

Julie laughed and promised.

She was feeling almost back to normal by the time Teresa appeared the next afternoon. After lunch, she had shampooed her hair in the shower, dried it quickly, and dressed in her warmest sweater and jeans. Her appetite had returned, so she figured she was healthy again.

Teresa came in, waving a mimeographed sheet. "Nominations for Princess. A few surprises in the competition, but nothing you can't handle. Here, take a look."

Julie waved her to a seat in the kitchen break-fast nook, brought the teapot, and poured the fragrant lemon-flavored tea. Then she settled opposite her friend to study the list with interest.

"Hey, I see what you mean. Pam and Sandy and — Mary Lou Montgomery! How about that?" She stared at Teresa for a moment. "You know, I wouldn't be surprised if she won."

"No way. You've got it all sewed up." The dark eyes looked thoughtful. "But Greg's campaigning hard for her. Did you know — ?"

Julie nodded. "Met them coming out of the library a few days ago. I felt kind of bad about it — no, not because of him. It was just that I wanted to get to know her better. She's a really neat girl. And I wondered if somebody would tell her about a few of his less delicate habits before — well, before she finds out the hard way like I did."

After a while, they went to work on the vocabulary list. Shortly before six, Julie insisted that Teresa leave, knowing she had to get ready to go to her grandmother's for dinner.

"You still don't have them all," Teresa said, frowning at the list.

"I know." Julie groaned. "It's like my mind's so slippery, nothing sticks. Everything just goes skidding off into space. Well, I'll hit it again before I go to sleep. Thanks, anyway. You really helped."

She made one more attempt to assimilate the material before she turned out the light that night. It had worked before, the midnight cram session. At least she retained enough to pass a test the next day.

This time, once she closed her eyes, she couldn't keep her mind on the dull details in those chapters or the terms on the list. For some reason, she kept thinking about Mary Lou and the nominations for Homecoming Queen and her court.

Would it mean as much to her as to Mary Lou? she wondered. New to Mesa Verde, still getting acquainted with the school and the local kids, the election as princess might be more important to the girl from Texas than Julie suspected.

She felt increasingly uneasy about her own chances. If she wanted to win — well, of course she did. Be honest about that much. Winning would be something solid and tangible. A Homecoming Princess could be sure people liked her, that she was popular and — a great person. Simple as that.

She voted the next day at lunch, hesitating for only a second before she checked off her own name. It would be silly not to vote for herself. At least, if she lost, she wouldn't have to wonder if one vote would have made the difference.

Miss Coleman had been very nice about the makeup test, scheduling it for Friday after school. Then she looked at Julie closely and shook her head. "Your face is thinner, dear. Not that it hurts when someone has the elegant bone structure you do. Marvelous bones in your face."

Julie had to struggle to keep from laughing. Trust a biology teacher to be interested in bones, even the kind in people. Live people.

Miss Coleman must have detected her amusement. "If you're heading for the theater, Julie, you'll find something like that can be an asset. The poor souls with pug noses and pudding faces won't stand a chance, not against people with bones like yours."

That night, Julie stared at her face in the mirror for a long time, twisting her head so she could study it from every angle. She turned away at last with a soft sigh. She couldn't see anything so wonderful about her bones. And the face was just a face, nothing exceptional about it.

She had intended to study once more for the biology test, but the first day back at school had tired her. She fell asleep over the book, waking just long enough to toss it on the floor and turn out the light.

A few minutes before the last bell the next afternoon, the results of the preliminary election came over the loud speaker. Julie stiffened as the Vice Principal paused, shuffling papers before she read the five names from the junior class.

"Paula Sutherland, Sandra Wiegand, Beth Oldham, Pam Newhouse and — Mary Lou Montgomery."

Muffled cheers and moans, a ripple of excitement swept the room, and several heads turned to watch Julie. She felt her cheeks burn as she pretended to listen intently. The Vice Principal finished reading the rest of the lists — in a maddening slow precise voice. She completed the last one seconds before the bell, time enough to add with patently phony enthusiasm, "Good luck, girls!"

A moment later, Julie jumped to her feet, assumed a cheerleader's stance, and exhorted the room in the unmistakable accent of Texas.

"Come on, let's *heah* it for Miz Montgomery!"

C H A P T E R 1 0

Julie reached her locker ahead of most of the crowd, anxious to get her books and meet the twins in the parking lot before people came around to sympathize. Or to gloat in one way or another with poorly disguised glee over her loss.

She felt a hand on her shoulder and whirled, then managed a smile when she saw Nick. "Hey, Nicko, it wasn't that big a thing. Don't look so — "

"It was a rotten ripoff, that's what it was." His eyes were grim. "Listen, it's all over school. That creep Greg, he did everything but stuff the ballot box. I wouldn't put that past him if he could figure a way to do it."

Julie shook her head. "Just forget it, will you? Those girls won fair and square."

"Like hell they did."

She stared at him. "I don't think I want to hear this. It's down the drain, Nick. How come you're not coming on with a little Band-Aid pep talk? You know, something like, how much difference will it make ten years from now?"

"Because I'm ticked off, that's why." As they made their way down the corridor, he put his arm around her shoulder.

Julie usually felt warm and cherished in the protective embrace of Nick's big arm. Today, she had to fight the impulse to shrug it off. Actually she didn't want Band-Aids or pep talks any more than she wanted sidelong glances and smothered snickers.

She concentrated fiercely on a pain somewhere behind her breastbone that made it difficult to breathe. Stupid, she told herself, to let something mean so much that it hurt like this when she didn't get it, especially something as mickey-mouse as a school election. Stupid.

"You know what he's doing?" Nick continued in the same angry tone.

"Who?"

"Greg," he said impatiently. "He put out the word. If Mary Lou wins, he throws a party for everybody in the junior class. His dad says he can hire the Fox and Hounds for the night, five-piece combo for dancing, the whole shot. *If* Mary Lou wins."

Julie stumbled on the curb before they crossed the grass divider into the parking lot. "Using her," she said softly. "To get back at me. She'd hate that."

"Yeah, well, I'm not too happy about it, either. You should have won the thing in a walk. When you didn't make it even as far as the first ballot, anybody can see somebody did a number on you."

She gave a brief laugh. "Thanks for the vote of confidence. But there were five girls on that ballot, Nick. How about Pam and Sandy and Beth and Paula? I haven't heard about any of their boyfriends campaigning for them against me." Gently, she disengaged herself from his arm and smiled up at him. "Look, I'm not about to go that route. Am I a sorehead? Probably. But paranoid? No way."

"You should have won," he insisted.

"I told you all along I had my doubts." She waved as she saw Teresa running toward them. "There just aren't that many people at M.V. who realize how adorable I am. Now you — you got taste, Charlie."

He sighed, then bent to kiss her. "As long as I got you, Babe — " He grinned at Teresa, then turned to run down the aisle of cars in his curiously graceful lope.

Teresa touched Julie's arm. "Sorry," she said. "You should have had it. I kept wondering why you doubted it for a minute."

It was time for painful truths. Julie winced. "I never thought I'd make it to the finish line," she said, "but I — I did figure I'd be on the first ballot. That kind of — that hurt." She added quickly, "Nothing I can't handle, though."

Tony had approached without her seeing him.

He said now, behind her, his voice quiet, "If royalty's your thing, Jule, you've been a thoroughbred in my book for a long time." He put a hand on his sister's head. "You and the kid here. So who needs elections to find out who's got class and who doesn't?"

"You make us sound like we're running at Santa Anita. I know we have long legs, but this is ridiculous — " The voice was a fair imitation of Phyllis Diller, but the laugh didn't make it.

Tony made a big deal of fumbling through his pockets for the car keys, though Julie suspected he knew very well where they were. She felt a wave of gratitude for the sensitivity he showed on occasion. By the time she got in the back seat, she had managed to blink back the tears.

An hour later when her aunt heard the news, she seemed to realize the extent of Julie's disappointment, though clearly not the underlying reasons. Her brown eyes flashed with indignation, however, as she muttered something about a "true count."

Julie was glad she hadn't told her that Greg was dating Mary Lou, and she hoped Roz would never hear anything about his campaigning tactics. There didn't seem to be much chance of that, though Julie was afraid Mary Lou would find out sooner or later.

She made a face at that unhappy thought.

Her aunt caught the involuntary grimace and misinterpreted it. "Well, it's no night to sit home and gloom about Watergate politics at good ole

M.V.," she said on a determinedly light note. "Let's go out on the town. How about Long John's for lobster?"

Julie groaned. "I should stay home and study for that makeup test tomorrow."

"Don't be ridiculous. You'll ace the silly old test."

Julie did feel a lot better once they had settled in the soft luxurious leather chairs at Long John's, one of her favorite restaurants. The waiters were good-looking college kids dressed in pirate costumes, and both the dining rooms had roaring fires in big fieldstone fireplaces.

She found herself relaxing in the warm, cheerful atmosphere. Her appetite back to normal now, she sat eagerly anticipating the fabulous food for which Long John's was famous.

Roz sipped her drink and launched into a wry account of a woman client she called the Dingaling Duchess. "I swear, she could find seventy things wrong with the Taj Mahal. What she wants is luxury, custom construction — the way homes were built in the thirties, say." She added with a sigh, "And prices from that era too. The woman's unreal."

Five minutes later, Julie eyed her, curious. "Hey, you're really pushed out of shape," she said at last. "You've been around the track with people like the Duchess before. How come you let her get to you?"

Her aunt looked at her for a moment, then gave a short laugh. "You're right. She reminded

me of Grandma Bailey. I noticed the resem-
blance, naturally, when she first came in the
office. But it was more than that, the same aura.
D.A.R., W.C.T.U charter member. I bet she's
the Philathea Circle Hospitality Chairman. . . ."

"The *what*?"

Roz nodded. "You have a lot to be grateful
for, sweetie. Things like that were very much a
part of my childhood, my growing-up years. My
mother and all the other rigid ladies from a
certain segment of society, middle-class, con-
servative — when I think of how they tried to
maneuver their daughters into the same narrow
little slots — the waste — !"

She gazed thoughtfully into the leaping flames
nearby. The light flickering across her lovely un-
lined face revealed a momentary tightness
around her mouth.

It was almost as if a resentment gradually
built up in her against the people who had
shaped her childhood, until she had to release
an unbearable pressure by talking about it, again
and again. Julie watched her, caught by the bitterness in her aunt's low voice. Knowing where
this conversation generally led, she knew as well
that it was hopeless to try to distract Roz until
she had said everything she wanted to say.

"I never bought it," her aunt said with acid
emphasis, "but Ann did. The whole business, all
the stupid standards and values, the rules and
restrictions. Mind-boggling. Your mother was a
lovely, warm, intelligent lady except for those

warped ideas, and they were programmed into her by the time she was in her teens." She lifted her glass to her lips, still staring into the fire.

Julie shifted uneasily in her chair. "She was happy," she said on a faintly defiant note. "I remember her that way. And in her pictures, she looked happy and — " She debated a choice of words. Contented? Satisfied? Yes, her mother had been a really together person, she was sure of that.

But Roz had already shrugged off the heavy mood. She shared a brilliant smile with Julie and the approaching waiter. "How can you be happy when you aren't free? The two of us, we're lucky, Babe. And here come our salads."

Julie ate a few bites and discovered she wasn't as hungry as she had thought. She hated it when her aunt zeroed in on Grandma Bailey, because invariably she turned to her sister Ann as a secondary target. She never denied her bitterness toward her mother. Yet, her sister had been a great deal like Grandma Bailey, as Roz so often declared. Was it possible then that — how did she truly feel about her sister? Subconsciously, perhaps, not even confronting that feeling? About Ann. And Ann's daughter. . . .

Julie straightened and pushed the nebulous, distressing thoughts away. As she turned to glance at the tables nearby, she saw a familiar face in a corner booth. "Oh," she said, pleased and startled. "There's Mr. Lawton."

Roz followed her gaze. "Interesting face," she murmured. "I'll bet he was a terrific actor. Can't you see him as — oh, one of the tormented people in something by O'Neill? Even Hamlet." She paused. "I remember you mentioned the child," she said then with a delicate undertone of distaste.

Julie looked again at the corner booth. Yes, the pleasant-faced woman sitting opposite Mr. Lawton reached now across the table to hand a cracker to the child beside him. Julie had a glimpse of a profile, short dark hair. A little girl, possibly nine or ten.

She drew in her breath as the child leaned forward to look at the fire. Strange. What were the visible clues to mental retardation? She had seen at a glance that the little girl was — different. But how? She stared at her plate for a moment, pondering the question.

The eyes, she decided at last. The expression in them or maybe a lack of expression — something missing, some vital spark of intelligence and personality. Those dark eyes she had glimpsed were dark in a tragic sense, as well, because they were curiously empty and lifeless for the eyes of a child.

Her aunt gave a slight shudder. "I suppose I shouldn't admit it, but I always feel a — a revulsion for children like that."

Julie looked at her, appalled. "It isn't as if she could help it." She heard the outrage in her voice and didn't try to soften it as she continued. "Any more than you could help being born with brown eyes or — or white skin."

Roz lifted her slim shoulders in casual acknowledgement of the rebuke. "I knew I shouldn't have admitted it," she said lightly. "There are people who are revolted by white skin, I daresay, perhaps with good and sufficient reason, in their view, anyway. No, but children like that — I can't help sensing a — something that isn't good and right and normal — like over-ripe fruit."

"That's a terrible thing to say!" Julie glared at her. "I sure hope you don't admit that to anyone else."

Roz laughed. "Are you uptight because of the little girl or because she belongs to your sainted teacher? And speaking of sainthood, are you quite sure he qualifies? I mean, anybody who goes around warning all the rest of your teachers that you have to keep to the mark or lose your auditing privileges — well, I have my doubts about the warm-hearted, generous Mr. Lawton."

Julie found herself wishing that she'd keep them to herself, but she managed to bite back her angry retort. It seemed an inordinate amount of anger, she admitted. Probably it stemmed from the fact that she had twice witnessed a rather impressive kindness in the teacher.

He seemed especially sensitive to the kids in class who were shy. In fact, in those early sessions, he made a point of discussing talented people in the theater who were still painfully shy, and those who suffered agonies of stage-fright even after years of performing.

Once, Julie watched with great interest as he

assigned a specific exercise to two students in his group who were still nervous and uncomfortable as the focus of attention. He told them the wind had slammed the door of their home closed, and they were locked out in freezing weather. Their ensuing pantomime permitted both to use their uncontrollable trembling as a part of the silent skit. Julie thought now, it had taken a very warm-hearted teacher to come up with something like that, but she didn't tell her aunt about the incident.

Roz seemed only too happy to carry the conversation by herself. "It's because he's strong," she said and nodded as if Julie had conceded the point. "Strong men are eternally fascinating. I suppose most women find a lot of security in that sort of thing." She sighed. "It would be a comfort in a way, not having to depend on your own strength twenty-four hours a day every damned day in the year. If I ever find a paragon like that running loose, I'll — " She broke off, glancing toward the corner booth as she noted Julie's renewed interest in the teacher and his family.

They were getting ready to leave. Julie couldn't seem to look away. She watched Mr. Lawton help his little girl with her coat and was glad later that she hadn't missed those brief seconds, even if it had been rude to stare. She had seen the expression on the teacher's face as he cradled the little girl's face in his hands, then looked up to smile at his wife.

Swallowing hard, Julie was glad to see the waiter approaching with their dinners on his tray.

"Yum," Roz said a few seconds later. "I must say, our young man is as good at his job as he is gorgeous to look at." She grinned at Julie. "Don't ever latch on to anything that beautiful, though. It's an everlasting fight for the mirror. Remember George? No, of course you don't. My first was a very foxy dude." She sighed. "I suppose I equated all those impressive muscles with strength."

"Listen," Julie said evenly, "if you ever did find anybody all that strong and secure, it wouldn't last five minutes. You're always saying you can't stand it if you don't get your own way. So how long is somebody really solid and together going to put up with that routine? Not twenty-four hours a day, day after damned day, he won't."

Her aunt laughed. "You may have stumbled upon one of life's little mysteries, sweetie. When it comes to women, anyway, the key word quite often is 'perversity.' What we want, we get, only to discover it's not what we really want, after all."

She added in the same ironic tone, "I'd give that some serious thought if I were you. You're so much like me, you're going to run into a lot of the same problems. Count on it."

Julie put down her fork. "I'm not as strong as you are," she said carefully. "I think I'm like those other women you're talking about. Looking for someone strong enough to — to help me be stronger."

Roz looked amused. "Perverse *is* the word. Honey lamb, if you were one bit interested in a strong guy, the proverbial squared-away solid citizen, you wouldn't be going with Nick Devore. You'd be head over anklebones about tall, dark, and infuriating Tony Martone."

Julie swallowed several scorching paragraphs with her next bite of lobster. For the duration of the meal, she said nothing. But her aunt, happily exploring a favorite topic, didn't seem to notice.

CHAPTER 11

Friday came wrapped in gray, brooding clouds that didn't disperse until early afternoon, chased across the sky by a cold biting wind. It proved to be a day fraught with disaster from the first moment when Julie broke two fingernails, snagging them on the blanket as she got out of bed. She had overslept and in her hurry to get down to the Martones on time, she forgot both her lunch money and the English homework that was already a week late.

In P.E. someone swiped the dollar Teresa lent her, but Julie decided not to report the theft. She had tucked the money in one of her shoes, but it was against the rules to leave money in the lockers, and she knew she wouldn't get any sympathy from Miss Varilla. The teacher had been cool since the incident at tryouts.

After school, Julie reported for the biology makeup test, took one look at the questions, and groaned aloud. She'd been afraid she'd do poorly, yet somehow she was unprepared for a wipeout. There had always been the chance she could fake it for a couple of essay questions. Words came easily to her, and a lot of words could sometimes obscure a very superficial knowledge.

Miss Coleman had not included any essay questions, however, not even a true-or-false section. The test called for specific information, so the teacher could see instantly whether or not a student knew the answers. Julie didn't.

She walked home under her own small black cloud, knowing she would have to sit through the Homecoming Game under any conditions, even if it rained. It did not, but Julie was glad she had worn her fleece-lined coat. In the cold night air, she felt sorry for the Homecoming Queen, a really nice blonde girl named Laney Purcell, and the three princesses, all in long dresses with no wraps over their bare arms and backs.

Julie's heart gave a little leap when the loud-speaker called out the names, and she realized Mary Lou had won. Then she was on her feet with the rest of the crowd, cheering as the old Caddy convertible with the queen and her court circled the field. The four girls, their arms full of flowers, looked lovely and happy. And very cold.

Watching, Julie felt a sudden warmth within surrounding the surge of excitement. Mary Lou looked great, red curls blowing around a face that sparkled with laughter as she waved to the packed stands.

I'm happy for her, Julie thought with a vast relief. It really wouldn't have been that big a thing. Win a few, lose a few, and she had lost to somebody neat. Somehow, it took the sting out of this particular loss.

The fact that the Mesa Verde team went down to resounding defeat didn't matter as much as it might have, either, because Nick covered himself with glory. With minutes to play, he carried the ball ninety yards for the only score that night. But he took the Viking humiliation hard.

Over hamburgers later, Julie tried to console him. "You said yourself we didn't have a prayer, Nicko. The Spartans are strong this year, and the Vikings didn't give you that much support."

"Forty-two to seven, wow." The blue eyes looked bleak. "I just didn't figure we'd get whomped that bad. Oh, well." He managed a faint smile as Teresa and her date slid into the booth.

"We can't stay long," Teresa said breathlessly. "I have to be in by midnight. Aren't you going over to the dance?"

Julie shook her head, partly in answer to the question, partly marveling once again at her friend's good-natured compliance with a curfew that applied even to homecoming dances. "We decided there'd be more action here." She grinned. "Look around you. A bunch of instant replays. Half the team with their chins dragging on the floor."

Teresa's date, a tall thin boy with owlish glasses and the unlikely name of Dugan Francis Dugan, smiled at her. "There weren't more than half a dozen kids from our class at the dance," he said. "They're saving themselves for the big bash at the Fox and Hounds." Teresa must have kicked him under the table, because he broke off, looking uncomfortable.

"It's okay, Dugan. I got the word." Julie sighed. "I just hope Mary Lou hasn't. It's so rotten. It'll just make people wonder if she would have won, otherwise. And how many kids would vote for her just to get to go to a dumb party?"

Nick emerged from his moody silence. "Enough to keep you off both ballots," he said firmly. "Enough so she won instead of you. It'll be a real trip, that party."

She shrugged and looked down to stir her coffee, thoughtfully. Greg could be a wild man at parties, she recalled, and hoped someone would warn Mary Lou. Oh, surely, somebody would have filled her in by now.

"Julie?" Teresa nudged her. "You haven't heard a word we said. How about getting an early start tomorrow to drive up to that place in the mountains? You know, the one Dugan's been telling us about where you can ride horses and hike, and there's a campground for picnics."

"Great. The four of us? Is this your Saturday off, Nick? . . . Oh, good." Julie brightened,

113

intrigued by the suggestion. "Let's get up really early and eat on the way so we'll have lots of time there. That sounds like fun, and this week's been such a drag."

When her alarm went off at six the next morning, the idea had lost a lot of its appeal, but her spirits lifted by the time she showered and dressed. Luckily, she had packed her share of the picnic lunch the night before. She was ready by the time Nick's old van turned into the drive.

An hour later, they stopped for breakfast, so ravenously hungry, the girls were threatening to raid the picnic lunch. The sun came out as they drove on, and Teresa and Julie sang for a while until they exhausted their repertoire. Tactfully, they avoided school songs for Nick's sake, although he seemed to have recovered his amiable disposition overnight.

It was a perfect day, full of sunshine and clear crisp mountain air. The two couples hiked for miles across grassy meadows and up gentle slopes into the trees. They devoured the picnic with newly sharpened appetites. Then for a couple of hours they rode lazy, sleepy-eyed horses who refused to be coaxed into a gait faster than a trot.

Julie hadn't laughed so much in a long time. She sat hugging her aching ribs, watching Nick plead with his fat black mount to move. At last, the mare rolled her eyes, made a whiffling sound of disgust, and ambled down the trail, a vignette Julie found hilarious.

They started back to Mesa Verde later than

they had intended, thanks to the slow pace of that horseback ride. Dugan said reassuringly to Teresa, "No sweat. We'll have you home by nine easy. Nick, that's the last gas pump for a while. You got enough to get us to the freeway?"

"Sure," Nick said. "Half a tank. No problem."

Five miles down the road, Dugan's sharp alarmed voice roused the girls from a drowsy reverie to see smoke pouring from the van's hood.

Nick pulled to the shoulder of the narrow winding road and cut the engine. "We've got a problem now," he said unnecessarily. "Everybody out."

A few minutes later, he told them, his face grim, "Broken fan belt. Of all the rotten luck. Ninety miles from nowhere too."

"Wow," Teresa whispered. "What'll we do?"

Nick took a deep breath. "We walk back to that store where they had a gas pump. And pray they're still open."

Dugan groaned. "It wasn't a garage. I don't think they'd have — "

"No, but they'll have a phone. Bad enough the two of us get stuck here overnight, but nobody's going to send up a flare about us. And Aunt Roz won't care about Julie once she gets the word. Teresa — that's something else again."

He looked at her and shook his head. "I'm sorry. Looks like Tony was right."

Julie stared at him. "What did Tony say?"

Teresa sighed. "He said the van, well, he didn't think it was in any shape for a drive like this."

She sounded awkward. "It's just a freaky accident, Nick. I mean, something like a fan belt, it could happen to anybody, anytime. Anywhere."

"Yeah, well, it happened to us here and now. I have a hunch your old man's going to take a dim view of accidents like this one. Maybe it was a dumb idea all around."

"Maybe," Teresa said softly, "but it was my idea, don't forget that."

"The two Tonys won't, for sure." Julie's voice was weary. "Okay, guys, let's start walking."

Nick retrieved a flashlight from the glove compartment, locked the van, and followed the other three up the road. Darkness closed around them long before they reached the country store. They walked single file in silence for the most part, the girls in the middle, already bone tired from the day's unaccustomed activity.

By the time they saw the welcome lights of the store, Julie was limping. With blisters forming on both heels, she had removed her shoes for the last couple of miles to walk in her heavy socks on the blacktop road. The soles of her feet soon were sore and aching, as well, from the uneven surface.

She and Teresa huddled in a small booth in front of the store and ordered coffee from a fat sullen woman in overalls and a heavy plaid shirt. A pot bellied stove gave off a comfortable heat, and both girls sat in a numb lethargy for several minutes.

Nick and Dugan returned then from a long consultation with a man loading beer into a huge refrigerator in back. "Two more coffees," he told the woman who hovered nearby, her eyes cold with disapproval.

Nick's mouth twisted as he watched her clump away. "The natives aren't too friendly," he said, his voice quiet. "They have a couple of cabins in back, and I guess they thought — well, we explained the situation and cleared the air, so —"

"There's a garage a couple miles beyond the spot where we broke down," Dugan interrupted. "Nick and I can spend the night in the van. And old Tom back there says we can make one phone call. We want to make any more, he says, we'll have to hike down the road to a public phone."

Julie made a soft incredulous sound. "Unreal." She straightened. "Okay, let Teresa make the call. Mama Angel can let my aunt know and your folks too, and — what's the deal? Will somebody come riding to the rescue?"

Dugan nodded and slid out of the booth, extending a hand to Teresa. Nick and Julie waited in glum silence, sipping their coffee. Julie couldn't help hoping that Tony wouldn't be available to come and get them.

She knew she was being petty and unreasonable and silly. They were lucky to have someone like Tony who might bail them out. They wouldn't be in this predicament in the first place, had Nick listened to Tony's advice. Still, it would be no fun driving home if he did the I-told-you-so number all the way to Mesa Verde.

With a scratch of weary resentment, she heard

in her mind Nick's casual indictment. *"Aunt Roz won't care about Julie once she gets the word —"*

She wouldn't, of course. But at least she wouldn't be saying, *now if you'd listened to me* — with half a dozen variations on the theme.

A few minutes later, Teresa came back looking relieved as she told them Tony was on the way. "I talked to Mom. Dad wasn't home yet." She sighed. "He'll be waiting up for us, though. You can bet on that."

Julie squirmed on the hard booth seat. "Does Tony have to tell him — you know — that he warned Nick about the van?"

Teresa glanced at her. Her voice was even. "He wouldn't tell him unless Dad asked."

And Big Tony would ask, all right. Julie let out a long breath and felt her heart sink. She watched indifferently as Dugan went to buy a pack of cards from a cluttered counter nearby.

She had lost count of the games of gin rummy by the time the Toyota pulled up in front. Tony said very little, however, and Julie noticed that he looked as tired as they did. She recalled guiltily that he put in a full day on Saturdays, as a rule, helping his father on the job or working around the house and yard.

Once they dropped Nick and Dugan off at the van up the road, Julie insisted on taking the front seat so Teresa could stretch out in the back to sleep.

"You're just as tired as I am," Teresa protested.

"No, I'm wide awake. I had too much coffee."

Several miles later, Tony flicked off the radio. "Music makes me sleepy," he said. "Talk to me."

Julie looked at his stern profile in the dim light from the dash, a profile that would have looked fine on an ancient Roman coin. "I'm not good company tonight," she said. "No songs or jokes or snappy patter."

"That's a switch. The real Julie? It's been a long time since I met the lady."

"Don't be nasty."

He glanced at her. "It's the truth," he said simply. "You're hyper these days, always *on*. Sometimes I wonder if you aren't hiding on purpose behind somebody else's voice, the look on someone else's face. Do you still remember who you are?"

"I haven't the vaguest idea."

"Dammit, Julie! Do you have to sound so pleased about it? That's a really dumb thing to say."

She scrunched down in the seat as far as she could get with the restraint of the seat belt. "You don't want to talk, Tony. All you want to do is fight. So you're tired. I'm tired too. I'm sorry about the accident. I'm sorry you had to come and get us. But who needs a lot of heavy discussion about who I am and who's to blame?"

"Yeah, I wondered when you were going to get around to blaming people." His voice was heavy with scorn. "Poor Julie's got an aunt who lets her get away with murder. Poor Julie's got a biology teacher who won't. Poor Julie's blown the chance to sit in on the drama class. Listen, isn't it about time you stopped blaming other people for all poor Julie's troubles?"

"Will you get off my case?" She spit the words at him. "That's always your trip, Tony, playing God, all righteousness and virtue. You make me sick."

"No," he said in the same low fierce voice, "that's my line. When I see somebody with your potential, wallowing in self-pity — "

She pulled herself upright again, rigid with outrage. "*Self-pity*? Did you say — ?"

"That's what I said. Or you go off like a rocket when somebody *disappoints* you." His voice etched the word with acid.

"I'm not entitled to disappointment? I don't have a right to — ?"

"You have a perfect right. As long as you extend the same privilege to all those nice folks disappointed in *you*. Miss Coleman — you'll be lucky to get a C from her. And Mr. Lawton who's going to do just what he warned you he'd do — boot you out of his class. And Teresa and Angel. And me. How the hell do you suppose we feel?"

"Why would I — ?"

He supplied the word she had managed to bite back. "Care? Well, that's another good question, I suppose. But I think you do care, Jule, because you know we care about you. We're the only ones around who'll give you any guidelines, who want you to measure up." He gave a brief laugh. "Though I'll have to admit I'm the one who gives you all kinds of hell when you don't."

"Easy for you, isn't it, to sit and judge?" she said bitterly. "You've got a family, people helping you — even if Big Tony does come on like Genghis Khan sometimes with ninety-nine stupid rules." She added on a sour note. "Ninety for Teresa and nine for you, naturally."

"Who said anything about it being easy?" he asked, ignoring most of what she'd said. The words poured out of him as if he'd rehearsed them all the way down to pick them up, releasing them now under the pressure of anger. "No guidelines? You had your parents for ten years. Didn't they teach you anything? Why can't you give yourself guidelines? You aren't what other people make you, anyway. You're the kind of person you make yourself."

"Will you shut up?" she said, furious. "Will you kindly just shut your mouth?"

A long silence. In the back seat, Teresa coughed in her sleep and turned over.

"Are you crying, Jule?"

"I *never* cry."

"Maybe you should."

"Why? Because I'm a girl? Do *you* cry?"

"I have." He laughed. "I'm Italian, remember? When my Grandmother Martone died, everybody cried — my father, my uncles — And don't forget, no matter what you think of Big Tony, I'm half Mama Angels's son too. She sort of — tempers things in our family."

"She goes along with Big Tony most of the time, if that's what you mean."

"A lot of the time," Tony said, "not most. Well, a lot of the time she thinks he's right, or it's something that doesn't matter much, that won't hurt Teresa and me. She's a strong lady, Jule, strong enough to let my father be strong — when he needs to feel that way."

She stared at him. "And how about you and what you need, what you want out of life? Is she going to let your father make that decision too?"

"It isn't his decision to make," he said quietly. "Or hers. It's mine."

CHAPTER 12

It was almost midnight when Julie let herself into the dark, quiet house. A night light had been left on in the hall, but her aunt had gone to bed. Julie had expected that, of course, just as she had been certain that both of Teresa's parents would still be up, waiting.

She felt flattened emotionally after the long drive and the low-voiced furious exchange with Tony on the way. It hadn't helped that she was physically drained as well, even before the trip home. She stood under a warm shower for a long time, hoping some of the aching weariness would wash away. From the top of her head to the soles of her bruised feet, she felt tired and sore.

When she finally settled herself to sleep, she realized that she hurt even more inside. Fragments of Tony's blunt accusations still burned through her mind.

" — *about time you stopped blaming other people for all poor Julie's troubles — wallowing in self-pity — give yourself guidelines — you're the kind of person you make yourself —* "

She squeezed her eyes shut, but that only evoked a vivid mental picture of his frowning profile, mouth set in exasperation. Opening her eyes, she peered at the shelf with her parents' pictures, though the details of those smiling faces were lost in shadow.

"Is he right?" she whispered, and the echo murmured inside her head. *Right, right, right —*

Yes, she had blamed other people. Certainly, she felt a growing ambivalence about her aunt. She loved Roz, appreciating the extent of her generosity in taking a ten-year-old to raise. Then why couldn't she accept the fact that Roz, with no children of her own, had done the best job she knew how to do with her niece? Given that lack of experience and a deep resentment of certain aspects of her own childhood, how could she have acted otherwise?

Self-pity, Julie thought, and winced as the ugly words scraped once more at the hurting place inside. *Poor me. Because you died, Mom and Dad, and left me all alone. Why did you go away and leave me when I needed you so much?*

Her eyes stung as she stared at the shelf across the room, though the picture faces were clear in her mind. They hadn't looked like that, she thought, not really. Her thoughts veered away from that last journey in the car, from that last day. No, better to go back to the time when they lived in San Diego in the redwood house, a miniature version in a playhouse by the garage that her father had built for her. What had they looked like then? What had they been like, Ann and Phillip Enright, the young couple who would never grow older than the bland smiling likenesses captured by the camera?

Across the years, her father's voice spoke once more in the tone that discouraged argument. "No, Julie, you can't stay up five minutes longer. You're tired and cross right now."

Then her mother, in an equally firm voice, "I don't care what Kathleen's mother lets her do. I am not Kathleen's mother, I am your mother."

Julie smiled to herself, amused as she experienced once more the emotions of that eight-year-old, arguing, pushing against the limits set by the implacable adult world. But there had been a certain security, an enormous comfort in the awareness that those boundaries existed, that her parents cared enough to protect her, to do what was best for her.

"You know we care about you," Tony said in her mind, " — want you to measure up." And again, "Why can't you give yourself guidelines?"

"He's an MCP," Julie whispered to the pictures on the shelf. "The super C.B. of all time. Tall, dark, and infuriating. Aunt Roz was right, you know? He is strong. Maybe that's why he drives me up the wall. He doesn't just want me

125

to measure up, he's going to yell and holler and beat on me until I — until I — " She closed her eyes and allowed herself one quick peek into memory, wondering again about that kiss, about the new and scary thing that flared between Tony and her in those brief moments. Then she slid into the warm nothingness of sleep undisturbed by dreams.

Roz greeted her with a wide grin the next morning. She sipped coffee, her eyes smiling at Julie over the rim of the mug. "So you did make it home last night. I figured it might have been a switch on the old we-ran-out-of-gas routine."

Julie shrugged, unsurprised, but unable to quell a slight prickle of irritation. She poured orange juice from the pitcher on the counter. "You know that wouldn't work with Teresa's parents. Bad enough that the fan belt really did break. The poor guys had to spend the night in the van."

"Mmm. Poor Teresa too. Will she be grounded for the next six months?"

Julie helped herself to eggs and sausage on the stove and sat down in the breakfast nook. "For getting in after curfew? A week probably." She picked up her fork and looked at Roz. "I'm going to take myself out of circulation, too, for a while. I need the time to study for one thing. I bombed on that makeup test Friday." She sighed. "When report cards come out this week, well, I told you what might happen. I can forget about the drama class till next semester."

Her aunt frowned. "You're going to throw in

the towel? Just like that? You're pretty good at talking your way out of trouble. Isn't it worth a try?"

Julie shook her head. "No, Mr. Lawson told me what to expect. If he didn't follow through, if he was the kind of teacher I could do a job on, I don't suppose I'd respect him as much."

Roz laughed. "Never stopped you before, not until you took your best shot."

"Maybe it never meant as much before. This is — different." She chewed for a moment, swallowed, then nodded, one short firm jerk of her head. "It's all tied up in the way I feel about myself. Can you understand that? When you work really hard on something, Roz, on one of your package deals, say — " she leaned across the table, an urgent note in her voice " — and it goes through because of everything you put into it, well, isn't that a great feeling? Sure, the money's good too, but isn't the most important thing the way you feel about yourself?"

Roz looked amused. "I've never had any ego problems if that's what you were getting at in that impassioned speech. No, I take that back. Not since the day I left the old homestead — " she shuddered delicately " — I hate to think how many years ago. So what're you driving at, Babe? Knocking yourself out in school in some silly class that won't mean a thing six months from now, knuckling under to a teacher who's so rigid, it's idiotic — how's all that going to make you feel better about yourself?"

"I'm not sure," Julie said slowly. "I don't

know how to explain it. Maybe if I can be certain when I get something that I — that I earned it, that I deserve it — I just figure it might mean more to me. I might learn something." She brightened. "Maybe you can tie all that together in one word. Discipline."

"Heaven help us all," her aunt said in a soft wail. "Next thing you'll be hitting me with the blessings inherent in the Puritan ethic. There's a gleam in your eyes that I've seen before." Her voice sharpened. "Julie Ann Enright, who's been brainwashing you? Tony Martone? He went to get you last night, didn't he? And then he did the pure and noble number on you all the way home. Poor *baby*. Let me iron out the kinks in a hurry before you're warped for all time."

She looked genuinely alarmed when Julie burst out laughing. "You look — for a moment, you looked exactly like your mother! A throwback, that's what you are. Worse than perverse. I've given you freedom, and here you are opting for chains and solitary confinement."

"No way." Julie smiled at her. "Listen, Roz, you're fantastic at your job, right? Out there every day beating the guys at their own game, isn't that the way you put it?"

Roz looked grim. "You better believe it."

"So aren't you knocking the very thing that makes you a smashing success? Discipline?"

Her aunt stared at her. "It rarely slops over into my personal life, sweetie. You may have noticed I'm a far cry from a tidy organized hausfrau. And if you think I'd change places

128

with somebody who is, your Mama Angel for instance, think again."

Julie reached for the slim brown ringless hand close to her own. "Somehow, I can't picture you finding fulfillment in pasta — or putting up with Big Tony for five minutes."

"Well then?"

"But she's happy."

Roz made an impatient gesture of dismissal. "Happy? What's happy?"

"Not the same thing for everybody, that's for sure. I used to think — " She paused, recalling long earnest discussions with those pictures down the hall. How important it used to seem, she thought, being popular, the cute funny girl always good for a laugh, too often at someone's expense. And after all, what difference did it make what people thought about a personality she assumed as easily and quickly as she slipped on a sweater? She knew the person underneath was someone else entirely. Somebody she didn't like very much, as a matter of fact.

Now she found herself paraphrasing Tony's words. "You make your own happiness, I guess. And if it's not the same thing for any two people, maybe it's pretty important to find out as soon as you can what it is in your own case."

She thought dully, but first you had to find out who you were. And if you didn't like what you found, how did you go about changing yourself?

So far she'd disappointed a lot of people. This morning, with the best of intentions, still grop-

129

ing for answers, she had managed to disturb her aunt, as well. As she cleared the table and loaded the dishwasher, she felt Roz watching her, the brown eyes puzzled.

During the rest of that day and the week that followed, Julie discovered it was one thing to feel virtuous momentarily in concluding the time had come to shape up her life. Maintaining the emotional momentum of those high-minded moments of decision was another thing.

Nick called late Sunday afternoon, in no mood to accept her reason for canceling their usual movie date, not when it was clearly a manufactured excuse.

"You've got to *study*?" A short humming silence. "Come on. Are you mad about last night?"

"Why would I be mad?" With an effort, she laughed lightly. "You guys are the only ones with anything to complain about. I figured you might want to hit the sack early tonight."

"Well, you figured wrong. I want to see you."

"Teresa's grounded for a week."

"So what else is new? I'm not asking Teresa to go out. And I know your aunt. She didn't care how late you came in. And you aren't that hot to hit the books tonight. So put it right up front, will you? What's the problem?"

There was more, the closest thing to a fight they'd had yet. Nick said good-bye and hung up at last, sounding cross and unconvinced. Julie went to sleep feeling faintly martyred. She had studied for several hours, memorizing the biology vocabulary list, reading all the chapters in the textbook covered in class so far. She knew the answers now to all the questions on the test. Too late to do her grade any good, of course.

She told herself wryly, the new regime didn't seem to make a lot of sense so far. Aunt Roz had acted as if Julie were considering resigning from the family. Nick was obviously uptight, and for what? So Julie could fill her head with facts about a subject she detested, facts she would forget just as quickly as possible once the semester was over. Crazy.

Miss Coleman stopped her after class to say quietly, "I'm sorry about the grade. I know how much it meant to you, but — "

"It's okay." Startled, she noted the teacher's eyes were suspiciously bright behind those absurd half glasses. Imagine, Miss Coleman caring that much about her grade. "I have to tell you, you were right about science not being my favorite thing," Julie said, "but I won't blow it again like I did on the test."

The teacher looked at her for a moment. Then she nodded and, with her quick warm smile, turned away.

Julie hurried to her next class, pondering the brief moment of satisfaction. It had been enough to make up for almost everything that had gone before.

CHAPTER 13

She gathered grades in each class that day, the C in biology which she deserved, B's which she did not in U. S. History and geometry. There was even an A in English which might be credited toward her entertainment value during that hour, though it hardly reflected academic progress.

In sixth period P.E., she gritted her teeth as she glanced at the slip of paper. Then she caught her breath. Miss Varilla had given her an A in the class with an accompanying C in citizenship.

Struggling with mixed emotions, pleased surprise, and a measure of guilt, she was not aware of the teacher's approach until she heard the husky voice behind her.

"Enright? You feeling okay?"

"Sure. I'm fine."

Miss Varilla studied her, the gray eyes cool.

"You've been rather subdued lately. I just wondered." She looked at the paper in Julie's hand. "Were the grades in here what you expected?"

Julie felt her face grow hot. "No," she said, then added on impulse, "I figured you'd really lay it on me. And I wouldn't have blamed you. I thought — "

"You were wrong." The teacher gave her a faint smile. "You earned both grades, Enright, fair and square. I've watched you work in class, and you're good. You may goof off, once in a while, but you're not lazy. I only hope — well, I'd like to see some of that drive, that coordination, channeled into other areas."

"You want me to shape up." It was not a question, but a statement.

"Uh — yes. Exactly."

Julie grinned. "I'm working on it. Thanks, Miss V."

The day seemed endless, but she did not welcome the sound of the last bell. The most painful confrontation was yet to come, and her stomach went cold and hollow every time she thought about talking to Mr. Lawton.

A dozen times, she played the scene with the teacher in her mind, coming on with cunning excuses, abject apologies, fervent promises, even tears. A dozen times, she recalled her aunt saying lightly, "You're pretty good at talking your way out of trouble. Isn't it worth a try?"

When it came down to it, in the echoes of the final bell, Julie didn't head for her locker. She went toward the gym, running, dodging around the kids streaming from the rooms along the corridor.

She saw him crossing the grass, walking toward the double doors. He smiled as she came up to him. "Enright. How's it going?"

"Not very well," Julie said, a little breathless from her fifty-yard dash across campus. "It's — my grades."

His smile disappeared, but he said nothing, curiosity flickering in his eyes. They narrowed as he tipped his head back to observe her down the patrician nose she had admired so many times.

She thought with a sudden flash of insight, he was waiting for an excuse. He had heard them all. Now, he was wondering with that wry humor of his what she'd try on him. He might laugh. There was an outside chance he'd accept her version of the situation. Yet, suddenly, she knew the most important thing was the way Mr. Lawton felt about her.

"I'm sorry," she said. "You gave me a chance to sit in on your class, and I loved it. I learned a lot."

He raised his eyebrows in a silent question.

"Well, I blew it," she said. "I knew a test was coming up in biology, and I just didn't study. So I got a C. I know that means I can't sit in with your class anymore. I — I wanted you to know that I've learned something."

Abruptly, she ran out of breath. She told herself fiercely, with all her practice in voice control, she had blurted out that dumb little speech with no rehearsal, no polish whatsoever. How could he pick up anything but a total lack of concern? He certainly wouldn't think she cared a whole lot about the opportunity he had offered, not when she bobbled it a couple weeks later.

He said, his voice quiet, "You want another chance."

Julie's head went back. "No! Oh, I don't mean I wouldn't want it, but like I said, I've learned something. About discipline, about me. Maybe about you too. So I knew you wouldn't go back on what you said to give me a second chance. But what's sort of neat about that is — " She paused, startled, because Mr. Lawton had begun to laugh.

"You don't happen to be taking a class in psychology, do you, Enright? Because if this is a reverse approach, it's — um — it's a classy one, all right."

"You wouldn't believe the number of things I thought up to say to you." Julie's voice was flat.

"Oh, yes, I'd believe it. Assuming you changed your mind about the entire list, I'd like to know — why?"

She sighed. "I wish I could tell you. I'm not clear about — well, about me, I guess."

He stood for a moment looking at her. "You may have learned a lot more than anybody else in my group," he said. "I'll be waiting for you, Julie, with a great deal of interest. I have a hunch what you're groping for right now is your own voice. Think about that."

He turned toward the door, then glanced back to smile at her. "Thanks," he said. "There's something I want you to know too. You haven't disappointed me."

Julie walked slowly back to her locker, hugging her books to her chest even as she held tightly to the warmth of those few minutes. It seemed as if Mr. Lawton had given her a marvelous clue to his secret. It was implicit in something he said. All she had to do was reach out and grasp it.

She rounded the corner into the locker area, her steps slowing. But she saw immediately that Nick was not waiting for her. He must have wondered why she hadn't come to meet him as she always did.

Later, she told herself. She could explain, soothe his ruffled feathers, write him a funny poem to make him laugh. Later. At the moment, she felt nothing but relief that she would have time to examine everything Mr. Lawton had said while it was fresh in her mind.

Someone touched her shoulder, and she whirled impatiently. Then she smiled as she saw the tall slender redhead.

"Oh, hi, Mary Lou."

"It's been a day, hasn't it?" The soft honey-smooth voice sounded rueful. "I mean, I haven't just covered myself with *glory*. How 'bout you?"

Julie shrugged. "What I expected. A few surprises, maybe. Oh, well, look at the new fields they're opening up for women. We can always drive a truck or collect garbage, right?"

"Wrong." Mary Lou laughed. "I nevah could get up that early." She hesitated. "Got an hour you could spare, Julie? I was hopin' we could grab a Coke and — and *talk*?"

Julie's heart sank. The request couldn't have come at a worse time, just when she wanted to be by herself to do some serious thinking. But she couldn't refuse, not with Mary Lou watching her with intent, anxious eyes. Clearly, she needed to talk to someone, a feeling Julie knew all too well. She was lucky enough to have Mama Angel and Teresa to help her get squared away.

"Sure," she said. "Let me get my books — and my filthy gym clothes." Recalling the unexpected A from Miss Varilla, she smiled to herself as she unloaded the top shelf of her locker.

Later, over hamburgers, the two girls compared notes on their grades. At last, just as Julie had begun to wonder what it was Mary Lou wanted to discuss, the other girl took a deep breath and spelled out her problem.

"I wanted to talk about that big ole fancy *hoedown* Greg's plannin'. Tomorrow night. I reckon you heard?"

Julie nodded. Sucking on a piece of ice from her Coke, she watched Mary Lou, curious.

"I told Greg I wanted you to come. Specially." The soft slow voice underlined the word.

"Oh. I — I hadn't planned — "

"That's what he claimed you'd say. But I told him, no harm in askin', if he wouldn't mind. And I was certain sure you wouldn't be silly about goin'. It's nothin' but a fun thing for all the kids and real *sweet* of Greg's daddy doin' it. But, Julie, I mean it. I do specially want you to come. It isn't even a datin' affair, if that's a problem, Nick havin' to work that night or somethin'." She leaned across the booth. "Say you'll come."

Julie hesitated. Then she nodded once more. "Okay. I always had the idea we could be — we could be good friends."

Mary Lou smiled. "I jus' have the idea we already *are*, so let's don't be silly about — othah friends we may have. Okay? I mean, you bein' so kind that day in biology, and jus' *outstanding* about the Homecomin' election. Not many girls would be sweet and understandin' about a thing like *that*, you know?"

She sighed. "I'm tickled that you'll come." For a moment, the green eyes studied Julie soberly. "There's one othah thing. I don't *like* askin' you, makin' you feel you're obliged to answer. I do want you to know that. But I told my mothah, so many of the girls have jus' *hinted* around the subject, nevah comin' out flat in so many words. I said I figured I could ask you, and I'd eithah get the truth or — " one slim hand gestured lazily " — or you'd tell me straight out that you'd rathah pass. You wouldn't *hedge* about it."

Julie looked down at her glass thoughtfully and shook the remaining ice in it. "Something about Greg?"

"That's exactly it." Mary Lou sounded pleased. "I knew it. I knew you wouldn't fuss around the edges."

"Maybe it's just my guilty conscience talking." Julie looked up. "Late in the game, at that. I wondered if it wouldn't be a good thing if I told you — and then I talked myself out of it. Mainly because it can get kind of sticky, leveling with another girl about — about somebody you used to date."

Mary Lou rolled her eyes. "Tell me about it." She gave a brief laugh.

In the echo of the soft comfortable sound, Julie thought, amused, she even laughed with a Southern accent.

"I reckon that's just what I'm askin' — for you to tell me. What is it they're all hintin' at when they say he's a — he's a devil at a party?"

Julie groaned. "I might have known. Well, I did know, but I was sure somebody would tell you." She made a face. "He drinks too much," she said evenly, "and then he gets — uh — stubborn about driving home."

A short silence.

"I don't care much about the job of telling you that," Julie added awkwardly, "but if anything happened — well, I've got enough to carry around without something like that on my back."

Mary Lou moaned. "Don't we all? Thanks. I sort of figured it might be something like that. I picked up a few things. And if there's one shortcomin' my daddy purely hates and *despises*, it's somebody hittin' the bottle and then gettin' behind the wheel of a cah. Specially when that somebody is drivin' his own beloved *daughtah* — "

139

She grinned at Julie, doused her french fries with catsup, and shoved the bottle across the table.

Julie shook her head and drawled, "Nothin' mo *revoltin'* then all that red *goo* on a bunch of frahs!"

Mary Lou laughed, delighted. "Is that actually how I sound? I get the *inflection,* but — "

"You never really hear your own voice the way it sounds until you hear it on tape." She paused as Mr. Lawton's voice said in her mind, *"I have a hunch what you're groping for right now is your own voice — "*

That was it, she thought, bemused. Everyone had a voice, sometimes several voices. The thing was to find the one that most perfectly spoke for you. No, it wasn't that simple. She thought wearily, even when you found that unique voice, you still had to come up with the courage to use it.

CHAPTER 14

Shortly before eight, Julie swept into the living room and did a slow turn in front of Roz. She had borrowed her aunt's long plaid skirt, although she wore a fitted red velvet top with it. Roz had the figure for a slinky black jersey halter. More up front than she'd ever have, Julie thought with faint regret.

"Yeah," her aunt drawled now on a note of approval. "Red's good on you. Brings out your coloring. Your eyes look bluer, and your hair looks even lighter." She watched her niece sit briefly in a chair, then get up to wander around the room before she perched again on the arm of the couch.

"What're you so antsy about? Do you think Greg might give you a hard time? I doubt it, Babe." She laughed. "He isn't apt to want to tangle with that young giant you're dating now.

141

Unless he's tanked — and I understand a few people have had a word with the management about this party. I don't think there'll be a problem with booze as long as you stay on the premises."

Julie turned to stare at her. "Did you — did you *know* Greg drinks too much?"

Roz lit a cigarette and gestured with it. "I figured it might run in the family," she said casually. "His father's a pretty good man with the bottle, I hear."

"And you let me date Greg, knowing he'd be driving me home?"

Roz shrugged. "The last time you went out with him, you announced rather firmly the next morning that it was his swan song whether he knew it or not. Remember?"

Julie nodded.

"You drove home that night, didn't you? The Corvette was out front till the following afternoon. How'd you manage that?"

Julie scowled. "Swiped the keys. Dumped him off at his cousin's house. Runs in the family, all right. Turkeys, both of them."

Roz studied the tip of her cigarette. "So who taught you the old key trick?"

"Mmm," Julie said. "Yeah. You did." She added, curious, "But didn't you ever worry?"

The dark eyes met hers briefly, and something sparked between them. "You come to mind once in a while." A short laugh. "When you wander in a couple hours after *I* get home from a date. When you take off in some dude's high-powered car, and he burns rubber before he's out of the driveway. I've been around the track a few times, myself. I know too damned well what's going on these days. Most of you kids have been dry behind the ears for a long, long time."

Julie looked at her. "You never said a word."

Her aunt made a muffled comment. "I heard enough words in my day to fill a lengthy book. I rebelled against every rule automatically. Maybe my parents meant well, tried to protect me. Case of overkill, I suppose. It got to be a bloody bore, that I know. Give me Brownie points, Babe. I tried to spare you."

She pointed a slender finger. "I've also given you a rather candid view of the world out there, about the male of the species and his — um — behavior. You are jolly well going to have to make your own mistakes and decisions at this point, Julie. Because I'm not about to warn or advise or lecture or preach or take you by the hand or — "

She laughed again, a brittle sound with a catch at the end. "Not with my colorful record, I'm not. It just never occurred to me that *you'd* rebel against — against the freedom I've given you. Because I meant well too."

She winced at the phrase. "I considered it the most fantastic gift I could give you, the only person in the world I — " She paused and said fiercely, "I'm getting maudlin in my declining years. Get in the car and go before I break down and blubber." She got to her feet and hurried from the room.

Julie sat for several minutes before she went to the kitchen and got the keys. Then she glanced at the child's slate which still hung from the side of a cupboard. Years ago, before she went off to play after school, she had used it to write notes to Roz. Now, she took it down, rummaged in the junk drawer for a piece of chalk, and scrawled a message. Then she propped the slate in front of the coffeemaker and went out the back door.

When her aunt went to the kitchen later to refill her coffee mug, she would find a reminder of those early years when Julie first came to live with her. Because the message was the same one a ten-year-old Julie had often written. "Gone out to play. Back soon. I luv U."

Several blocks from the house, Julie reviewed their curious conversation. Would she ever get to the point where she could feel she truly knew another person? Would everyone in her life be capable of surprising her at some stage? She sighed. Her aunt might be considered the person closest to her in many ways. Yet she had just revealed a side of herself Julie had never seen before, had never even suspected.

Roz *worried*, about her. Even more shocking, a few minutes ago, she had been close to tears, the very strong lady who considered tears a sign of weakness, rarely worth the wear-and-tear on a makeup job.

The light up ahead turned red. Julie braked

sharply and pulled her attention back to her driving. She glanced at her watch and saw that it was a little after eight. She sighed again. Nick hadn't been able to get off work tonight, after all, and this was Teresa's last night on restriction. Tony had promised to get to the party around eight. She had turned down his offer to pick her up, as a matter of fact, knowing he'd be taking a date. It seemed simpler to go by herself. If things did get sticky, she could leave without disrupting anyone's evening.

Minutes later, she pulled into the parking area beside the Fox and Hounds, a lushly landscaped place constructed in someone's conception of an English country home. She didn't see the Toyota as she drove slowly up and down the aisles and pulled at last into a corner slot. She could see the entry lane from there, so she switched off the engine and settled herself to wait, already regretting her promise to attend the party. If it had been anyone but Mary Lou —

Headlights swung in from the street, and a car came toward her. With a sigh of relief, she saw that it was Tony. He parked, got out, then grinned as he saw her under the overhead floodlight. For a moment, he appraised her outfit.

"Far *out*."

Julie laughed and responded in the routine they had considered hilarious as thirteen-year-olds. "Hi, sailor, new in town?" She realized then that he was alone. "Where's Shirley?"

"Flu." He fell in step beside her. "Poor Shirl. She's running a fever. Plus being steamed about

145

missing the party tonight. She may make the *Guinness Book of Records.*"

Julie glanced at him. "You sound remarkably cheerful about it."

He shook his head. "I'm sorry she's sick," he said, not sounding overly grieved. "But we're coming to a — a parting of the ways, I think. No big thing. We'll be very sensible about it and have a long serious talk. At which point, she'll say she thinks it would be best if we 'started seeing other people.' And I, after a suitable period of mourning — say fifteen to twenty minutes — will agree."

He held the door for her, and Julie stepped into the shadowy high-ceilinged entry. She paused then in front of the massive inner door.

"Is that the way it works? You're letting her save face?"

"Why not?"

She nodded. "That's nice."

"Doesn't have to end in a free-for-all, you know." He sounded amused. "Especially when you reach the point where both of you want to split. You don't feel much but relief. Who wants to have a big fight and slice each other?"

She looked up at him. And for a few seconds, she was aware of nothing but the curious expression in his eyes. Her breath caught in her throat as he made a slight movement toward her.

Abruptly, the inner door swung open. A laughing couple brushed past, bringing with them a wave of warm air and the sound of music and voices. The strange moment passed, and Julie preceded him into the restaurant, head back, smiling.

The tables in the big dining room were already crowded, people three deep at the long bar, ordering soft drinks and snacks. A combo in the corner played a Manilow medley for the couples jammed together on the small dance floor.

Julie gestured toward a back room, not even trying to make herself heard over the din.

"Find a table," Tony said, bending close to her ear. "Want a Coke?"

She nodded and turned to make her way through the crush. Spotting some of the neighborhood kids just leaving a booth, she waited for them to make their way through the tables, then headed for it.

"Hey, Julie, who're you with?" It was a tiny little girl they called K.C. Everybody liked her, though she rarely stopped talking.

"Tony Martone. Nick had to work."

K.C. grinned at her. "Hold the space. We'll be back. Five minutes on the floor is all we can take. I tell you it's — " Her high voice faded as she hurried out of the room.

A moment after she sat down, Julie looked up to see Greg and Mary Lou approaching. Greg's face was flushed, and his eyes were feverishly bright. He greeted Julie with unaccustomed enthusiasm.

"Hey, glad you came! Some party, huh?"

At his shoulder, Mary Lou gave Julie a radiant smile, then shrugged and followed, Greg's hand around her waist, as he crossed to talk to someone else.

When Tony arrived with their Cokes and a bowl of popcorn, he told her quietly, "Greg's flying already. You see him?"

Julie nodded. "I'll talk to Mary Lou before we leave, okay? She may want a ride home." Glancing around, she made a face. "It's so noisy, I'm going to get a headache. How soon do you think — ?"

"An hour or so. Not my thing, either. I hate parties where you have to yell." He got up and came around to sit beside her. "That's better. I want to talk to you." He leaned toward her and sniffed. "You sure smell good."

"Tony!" she wailed. But, unaccountably, she had to swallow her heart before a sound emerged. "Listen," she said then in a desperate attempt to restore normalcy, the jeering good-natured sparring between them, "that All-American nose of yours uses up a buck's worth of perfume every time you inhale. Just cool it, will you?"

She felt a faint relief when K.C. and the others came roaring back to join them. She couldn't help noticing, however, that Tony looked a little cross about it. Probably nobody else knew the signs, the way he had of whistling quietly and looking off into space.

It didn't last. Before long, he relaxed to laugh and talk with the others. Julie had just glanced at the clock, surprised to see that it was almost ten, when she heard a loud burst of laughter from the main room. The music had stopped, and Greg's boisterous laugh was unmistakable.

Tony turned to her, lifting one dark eyebrow. He made their excuses, turned aside the teasing protests, and steered Julie across the room in what seemed a matter of moments. But when they came through the archway into the wide hall, he led her in the opposite direction from the big dining room, into an alcove with phones on one wall, the doors into the restrooms on the other.

"Tony, what are you — ? I thought we were going to rescue Mary Lou."

"All in good time." He looked down at her, his hands on her shoulders. "Longest ninety minutes on record," he said softly. "Scrunched up beside you in that booth with your perfume driving me crazy and those characters telling elephant jokes."

She knew he was going to kiss her. She had known the moment he detoured her into the alcove what he had in mind. On one level, she didn't want it to happen. Yet at the same time, she must have wanted it because she lifted her face to meet him halfway.

She felt the same magical response as she had the first time he kissed her that night in his living room in front of the fire. She was not aware of the door opening behind them until she heard a familiar voice exclaim, "Excuse it, please. Don't let me interrupt anything."

Julie backed away, her face burning, in time to see a wide-eyed K.C. staring at her, then giggling as she scooted past the phones and around the corner. The motormouth of Mesa Verde High, Julie thought wearily. Of all people to catch her kissing Tony Martone, it would have to be the one girl totally incapable of keeping the incident to herself.

It would get back to Nick, of course. The afternoon of the tryouts, she had promised him she would never do anything to hurt him. Intentionally. Well, there had been nothing half-hearted about her cooperation just now, and she had known very well that kiss was going to happen.

Two hours ago, outside the door of the restaurant, she had known. So much for good intentions and noble resolutions and well-meant promises. Less than two weeks later, she found herself kissing Tony and enjoying it very much, indeed. Somehow the strength of her response seemed more demeaning than the fact that someone had witnessed it.

"Sorry about that," Tony muttered, then shook his head. "No, I take it back. Not sorry about it at all."

"I'd better leave," Julie said. "I shouldn't have come tonight. It was just — it was a big mistake." She moved toward the hall, then turned to say over her shoulder, "You'll see Mary Lou gets home? Or would you rather I — ?"

He leaned against the wall, watching her, no expression in the dark still eyes. "I'll take her home."

By the time she reached her car, it was difficult to swallow against the ache in her throat. It must be a little aften ten. By the time she got home, she could call the night number of the discount store where Nick would be helping unload a truck. He'd be home by eleven.

No, she wouldn't wait till morning to call. She might back away from the things that had to be said before she lost her nerve. That was the real danger, that she would chicken out, and someone else would get to him first with the news that she wasn't his girl anymore. She had to tell him how it had happened, and make it clear — oh, it was vital to make him understand.

She nodded firmly as she turned the key in the ignition. For several blocks, it played in her mind, over and over in various edited versions, how she would tell Nick, what she would say. Then as she began the descent from higher ground into the section of town known as Verde Valley, she realized with an inner jolt of panic that the headlights were reflecting now from a rapidly thickening fog bank.

She must be more than a mile from home, and only the final section led uphill in a gradual slope that might be clear. Julie felt cold perspiration trickle down her back, and her palms were slippery as she grasped the wheel. Heart hammering, she slowed to a crawl and looked desperately for lights, for some familiar landmark to orient her. This was a side street on the edge of town, as luck would have it, with long vacant stretches and no center line on the blacktop surface.

The right tire bumped over something, and

her stomach did a sickening flip. She had gone off the road, she thought, and stepped hard on the brake. But how far? Where was she?

She opened the window, then saw, horrified, that the fog was rolling into the car. Her stomach lurched once more, and she closed the window quickly. A faint oily smell lingered, and she scrubbed at her cheek where she had felt the touch of wet mist.

She turned off the motor then, but somehow she couldn't bear to touch the switch that would leave her isolated in darkness. Neither could she stand to watch the coiling smoky fog pressing in on the ineffectual twin beams from the headlights. After a moment, struggling with a tide of terror that rose to grip the back of her throat, she buried her head in her arms on the wheel.

CHAPTER 15

She was never sure how long she remained in that position, helpless in the grip of hysteria. The harsh sound of the sobs wrenched from her throat frightened her when she surfaced at last from the period of complete submission to emotion.

She raised her head from the wheel to curl in the corner of the seat, arms crossed in front of her, hands gripping her shoulders. Chin burrowed into her chest, the tears slipped from her tightly closed eyes to slide down her face and drip onto the sleeves of her coat.

So many tears, she thought. It was as if they came from a well within the hard knot inside, gradually easing the pressure, the unbearable tightening at the back of her throat. Silent tears now, so she could listen to the voices in her mind.

"She's just like you, Ann — that sunny even disposition — my two beautiful women —"

When had her father said that? Across the years, he spoke again in the fragment of memory, hauntingly familiar. Of course. That was how his voice had sounded, deep with a thread of laughter in it.

When she was small, had she been like her mother? Roz told her not long ago, "You're so much like me, you're going to run into the same problems. Count on it." And promptly contradicted herself a few days later. "For a moment, you looked exactly like your mother. A throwback, that's what you are — "

Julie found a handkerchief in the pocket of the coat, mopped her face and blew her nose. She was tired of the whole trip. *Who am I? I'm like this — I'm not going to be like that — that's the way I am —*

"Don't I have a choice?" she whispered to herself. "Dammit, I have a choice!"

Tony had told her that. "You're the kind of person you make yourself."

All right, perhaps you could choose the kind of person you wanted to be. But how could anybody running in place figure what that might be? Not with the kind of trained-monkey routine she did, for sure. Julie Enright, consistently cute, always working the same pitch, the voices, the jokes, the fast funny patter.

Please like me. That's what she had been saying over and over. And how could people decide whether or not they liked her when she never stopped clowning long enough to let them think about it?

Someone rapped on the glass behind her head, and she jerked around, heart in her throat for a moment before she saw that it was Tony. With the windows closed, deep in her whirling thoughts, she hadn't heard his car pull up behind her.

He opened the door, and she moved over to let him slide in behind the wheel. Then she was in his arms again, sobbing against his shoulder in a fresh burst of tears.

" — can't seem to turn them off," she gulped at last. " — *never* cry — must have stored up a g-gallon or so — "

"Sure," he said. "Sure you have." With gentle fingers, he smoothed the hair back from her face. "Feels good, doesn't it?"

She nodded, enormously comforted by the feel of the rough texture of his jacket against her cheek.

"Whoever said you have to be happy all the time? Nutty little Jule. Wouldn't be any contrast. If you weren't miserable sometimes, how could you tell when you were happy?"

"I sup-suppose." She moved away and took a deep breath. It was interrupted halfway by a small hiccup. "Oh, Tony. The fog — I was so *scared!*"

"I know."

She stared at him. "I'm off the road, aren't I?"

"Safest place you could be in this gunk. Thank God you left your lights on. Minute I hit this stretch, I thought — " He ended harshly, "I've been looking for you."

"But — but Mary Lou — ?"

"Her dad came to get her."

"Oh." Julie relaxed. "I figured you'd be taking her home and — and I guess I came unglued."

"Sure. Fog's scary. Even when it doesn't happen to be a personal phobia. For a couple minutes there, looking for you, I sort of freaked out myself." He leaned over to kiss her.

After a moment, she drew back to smile at him. "Poor Tony, between bailing me out and bawling me out — " She paused as he touched her face.

"I'd like to sign up for full-time duty," he said quietly. "If you feel the same way."

She had come to realize how much he cared, enough to tell her when she was out of line. Because he was truly concerned about her future, her happiness, about what kind of life she would have, what sort of woman she would be.

"That's one of those things I've known for a long time, Tony, how I feel about you. I just didn't know I knew." She curled her fingers around his hand as it rested against her cheek. "If you could wait — I have to talk to Nick and — and finish getting my head together."

He grinned at her. "Tony Martone is a patient man. Besides, I don't think you've got that far to go."

She reached up to kiss him again. It was exciting, the first faint awareness of where she was coming from. But more important, she knew now where she was going.